WRANGLING THE WANDERING RANCHER

BOOKS BY JODY HEDLUND

High Country Ranch
Waiting for the Rancher
Willing to Wed the Rancher
A Wife for the Rancher
Wrangling the Wandering Rancher
Wishing for the Rancher's Love

Colorado Cowgirls
Committing to the Cowgirl
Cherishing the Cowgirl
Convincing the Cowgirl
Captivated by the Cowgirl
Claiming the Cowgirl: A Novella

Colorado Cowboys
A Cowboy for Keeps
The Heart of a Cowboy
To Tame a Cowboy
Falling for the Cowgirl
The Last Chance Cowboy

A Shanahan Match
Calling on the Matchmaker
Saved by the Matchmaker

Bride Ships: New Voyages
Finally His Bride
His Treasured Bride

Bride Ships Series
A Reluctant Bride
The Runaway Bride
A Bride of Convenience
Almost a Bride

Orphan Train Series
An Awakened Heart: A Novella
With You Always
Together Forever
Searching for You

Beacons of Hope Series
Out of the Storm: A Novella
Love Unexpected
Hearts Made Whole
Undaunted Hope
Forever Safe
Never Forget

Hearts of Faith Collection
The Preacher's Bride
The Doctor's Lady
Rebellious Heart

Michigan Brides Collection
Unending Devotion
A Noble Groom
Captured by Love

Historical
Luther and Katharina
Newton & Polly

Knights of Brethren Series
Enamored
Entwined
Ensnared
Enriched
Enflamed
Entrusted

Fairest Maidens Series
Beholden
Beguiled
Besotted

Lost Princesses Series
Always: Prequel Novella
Evermore
Foremost
Hereafter

Noble Knights Series
The Vow: Prequel Novella
An Uncertain Choice
A Daring Sacrifice
For Love & Honor
A Loyal Heart
A Worthy Rebel

Waters of Time Series
Come Back to Me
Never Leave Me
Stay With Me
Wait for Me

WRANGLING THE WANDERING RANCHER

JODY HEDLUND

NORTHERN LIGHTS PRESS

Wrangling the Wandering Rancher
Northern Lights Press
© 2024 by Jody Hedlund
Jody Hedlund Print Edition
ISBN: 979-8-9896277-3-8

Jody Hedlund www.jodyhedlund.com

Scripture quotations are taken from the King James Version of the Bible.

This is a work of historical reconstruction; the appearances of certain historical figures are accordingly inevitable. All other characters are products of the author's imagination. Any resemblance to actual events or locales or persons, living or dead, is entirely coincidental.

Cover Design by Hannah Linder
Cover images from Shutterstock

Maisy Merritt kissed her sister's burning forehead. "Don't die while I'm gone, y'hear?"

Lying in the cabin's only bed, Nelly didn't move—not to blink or twitch or hardly even to breathe.

Maisy smoothed the young woman's hair back, the red strands tangled from the thrashing earlier in the week. If only to have the thrashing again instead of this deathlike stillness.

Urgency swelled inside Maisy—the same urgency that had been prodding her for the past day. Even though she didn't want to leave her sister alone, she had to go for help.

She straightened and peered through the slit in the gingham curtains. The dawn sky was beginning to lighten, and now she could see the boulders and fir trees surrounding the cabin along with the jagged peaks to the west.

It was time to go. She'd delayed long enough.

Letting the curtain fall into place, she shifted back to Nelly and allowed herself one last look. It might be the final time she'd see her sister alive.

Maisy wasn't fooling herself with wishful thinking. She knew the truth. Nelly had given up the will to live the day her newborn babe had died, so when the fever struck, she hadn't wanted to do a lick of fighting.

Her sister's sweet face was flushed with the heat that had been raging all week since shortly after the birthing. Even in her dying moments, Nelly was still so pretty, with her rounded face, wide cheeks, and pert nose with a smattering of freckles. Her long auburn lashes were almost a dark brown as they rested against her tanned skin, hiding away her eyes.

Everyone always remarked how much Maisy looked like Nelly, was a younger version except shorter and more petite. And it was true. The two of them shared the same bright-red hair, blue-green eyes, and freckles they'd inherited from their ma.

While they looked a lot alike, that's where the similarities ended. Nelly was three years older than Maisy's eighteen years, but sometimes it felt like ten, since Nelly had always been more serious and responsible, falling into a mothering role after their ma had died when

Maisy was only twelve.

In addition to becoming the caretaker of the family, Nelly was naturally docile and quiet and even-tempered. She'd married Glenn the way their pa had wanted her to. And she'd never gotten angry that Pa and Glenn were gone for weeks at a time with their mountain-man duties.

Maisy tossed a glare at the door, imagining her burly pa standing there. "If you'd come back when you said you were gonna, then maybe Nelly could've had the doctor looking after her by now."

But of course, Pa and Glenn hadn't returned in mid-September the way they'd planned. And now that October was well underway, they hadn't been here when Nelly had gone into labor.

After two miscarriages and a previous stillbirth, Nelly had held such high hopes that this time, everything would be different. Maisy was no midwife, but she'd been around enough birthings to know the way of things. And when the tiny girl had slipped lifelessly into Maisy's waiting arms, she'd done everything she could to revive the babe, but nothing had helped.

Nelly hadn't cried. But Maisy had shed enough tears for both of them, especially when she'd had to dig a hole in the ground and lay the babe in it.

Maisy swiped up the rucksack she'd packed with provisions for the two-day hike out of Arapahoe Valley to Breckenridge, the nearest town. If she didn't have any delays and didn't stop for long at night, she might be able to reach the doctor in a day and a half.

"Hang on till I get back." She squeezed Nelly's arm and waited, watching Nelly's face for some sign of understanding. But there was nothing, had been nothing for too many hours.

Reluctantly, Maisy let go and forced her feet away from the bed and across the one-room cabin that was crowded with the bed in one corner, stove in another, and a table with benches at the center. Every other available space was crammed full of clutter: animal pelts, snowshoes, metal traps, several rifles, oiled canvas, coils of rope, maps, and more.

Sprawled out in front of the door, Smoke raised his head, his pointed ears lifting to their full height, his keen golden eyes locking on her.

She nodded at the wolf. "Time to go."

Smoke pushed up, standing on his lanky legs, his thick fur a mixture of light gray and white, with patches of darker gray around his eyes and down his snout. He was on the small side, having been the runt of his litter when she rescued him. Even so, when he stood, he was taller than most dogs.

She grabbed her heaviest wool coat from one of the pegs near the door. She was already wearing corduroy trousers underneath her skirt, along with her thick leather boots and two layers of wool socks. During the three years she'd lived in the mountains of Colorado, she'd learned the unpredictable nature of the weather and knew better than to head out unprepared, especially in the autumn, when anything could happen.

After shrugging into her coat, she slipped on the gray Stetson Tanner had given her last year for Christmas. He'd teased her when he'd given it to her, telling her he was tired of her taking his coonskin cap whenever he came to visit.

It fit her head perfectly, as if he'd had it custom made just for her. Although he hadn't admitted to it, she suspected that was what he'd done, because he was always a thoughtful and generous friend.

Too bad he hadn't hiked up to see them recently. He could have helped her with Nelly or at least advised her on what to do. He probably would've gone to town for her.

But she hadn't seen him in weeks. Six weeks and four days, to be exact.

She could admit she was counting. With every new day that passed, the twist in her gut pinched tighter. It was the longest he'd ever gone between visits. Where was he? Had something happened to him? Or had he finally moved on from the area?

Tanner was, after all, a trapper and trail guide, just like her pa and brother-in-law. Such men were never content in one place for long. Three years was about the longest her pa had ever lived anywhere, which meant they'd be moving before too long. Probably the only reason they hadn't moved yet was because Nelly had been in the family way, and Pa had wanted her to have the babe first.

No doubt when he and Glenn came back from traipsing all over kingdom come, they'd pack up and head out first thing now that they didn't have the babe to worry about.

They might not have Nelly to worry about either . . . unless the doctor could get to her fast.

"C'mon." She patted Smoke on the head, then opened the door.

The chill of the night lingered in the dawn air along with the heavy scent of pine and woodsmoke. A fine layer of white glistened over everything, the first snow of the new season. It would melt off as soon as it was touched by the sun later in the morning. But for now, it sparkled real pretty-like.

The mountainside was cloaked in silence. Not even Roscoe the racoon was chattering at the early hour, and there was no sight of the little creature in the hollow fir tree behind the cabin where he made his home.

She'd rescued Roscoe too, just as she had countless other animals over the years. She always did her best to keep them only long enough to integrate them into the wild. Smoke, however, had refused to leave her. Every time she'd tried to make him go, he'd always come back.

Now that he was two and old enough to be on his own, she'd expected him to run off, look for a mate, and start his own pack. But he hadn't gone yet, wasn't even restless.

In the meantime, Smoke was a good companion.

The wolf loped ahead of her before pausing and growing still, his gaze on the woodland beside the cabin. There, in the thick growth, stood two elk, grazing on the low golden leaves left on an aspen. The creatures stopped midchew to stare, poised to run off.

Smoke lowered his ears, his predatory nature kicking in. She'd encouraged him to be independent and learn to hunt on his own. And at times he disappeared for a day or two to track and kill prey.

"Later," she said to him.

He watched the elk another moment before dropping his head and continuing along the trail that led down the mountain.

Even though the latch on the cabin door was broken, she made sure the door was secured, situated the rucksack on her back, then started after Smoke. If she'd had one of the horses, she could've made the trip in a day. But of course, Pa and Glenn had taken both, leaving her and Nelly stranded in the wilderness as usual.

"I will never, ever marry a mountain man." Her words echoed in the silence—words she'd declared often over the years. But this time, more so than ever, the frustration of living with mountain men churned inside her.

Smoke glanced back at her as if to commiserate.

"It's selfish, that's what," she said. "Running off and leaving the womenfolk behind to take care of the home and fend for themselves."

Nelly and Ma might have been content with that type of life and family, but not her. Maisy wanted a normal life with a normal home and a normal husband. And just as soon as she could branch off on her own and seek a normal future, she would.

For now, though, she wasn't at liberty to pursue what she wanted. Not as long as Nelly was alive. As responsible and adultlike as Nelly was, Maisy couldn't leave her alone whenever Pa and Glenn were gone.

How would Nelly hunt or fish or search for edible roots and berries—all the things Maisy had learned to do? How would Nelly survive for weeks without talking to anyone, not even the wild animal pets? And how would Nelly be able to handle questionable strangers passing by or even cantankerous neighbors like Lester Acker and his passel of sons?

At the edge of the level rise where Pa had built the cabin, Maisy stopped and peered to the river valley to the south. Had the sky been clear and bright, she would have been able to see the smoke rising from the Ackers' cabin downstream along the banks of Gold Bend River. As their closest neighbor, Lester was anything but helpful and had only stirred up trouble since claiming his land over a year ago.

Now that he had a small herd of cattle, he'd grown even more feisty and was gunning for Smoke something fierce. He'd already been up to the cabin a couple times over the past few weeks, accusing Smoke of terrorizing his cattle. Just last week, he'd warned her to keep Smoke away or else he'd kill the wolf.

She didn't think Smoke wandered as far as Lester's ranch. Or at least, she hoped not. Most likely the rancher was mistaking Smoke for one of the other dozens of wolves that lived in the area.

In spite of all her assurances, Lester seemed to think Smoke was behind every attack, as if the lone wolf was general of an army and coordinating offensives against him.

Unfortunately, Lester wasn't the only one with a vendetta against the gray wolves in the state. Most ranchers despised wolves because the creatures were killing more cattle since their natural food source of bison had become so depleted over the years.

Maisy understood the dilemma. Tanner had grown up on a horse ranch near Breckenridge and had explained the wolf problem during one of his visits. Even so, she hated the mass killing of wolves the same way she despised the mass killing of the buffalo.

Whatever the case, Maisy couldn't run off and leave Nelly to fend for herself in the mountains. If Nelly survived this stillbirth, it would take time to recover—maybe even weeks if the last one was any indication. Nelly would need her to be there more than ever.

With a sigh, Maisy started down the sloping path, planting each step carefully. Though the path was gravelly and rough, the thin layer of snow was still slick.

"Why couldn't you build down along the river like everyone else?" The grumbling question to her pa was loud in the early morning, causing Smoke to glance at her again.

While she loved the view from the clearing around the cabin, the hike up and down the mountain was treacherous even in the best conditions. But that was the way it was with her pa. He was stubborn and opinionated and always liked to be different.

"Look where that got you. A dead wife, and now possibly a dead daughter." She glanced around to the thick woodland that covered the hillside, half expecting him to come wandering down the mountain in his buckskin coat and leggings, his rifle slung across one shoulder and a stack of furs across the other.

She'd never doubted that her pa loved her and Nelly and their ma. He was an affectionate man and hadn't married again in the years since Ma's passing, claiming that he'd never love another woman half as much as he had Ma.

But what Maisy couldn't understand was, if he'd loved Ma so much, why had he left her for such long stretches? Why hadn't he wanted to be with her every day and night? How had he been able to live being away from her? Hadn't he realized how lonely and sad she got every time he left?

Maisy's foot slipped, and she grabbed the root of a spruce tree that was dangling from the sloping embankment on one side of the trail. On the other side, the vegetation and trees gave way to a rocky cliffside that bordered the river valley below.

She would have to descend the treacherous trail for another hour or so before reaching the level ground. From there, she'd be able to go much more rapidly, using the trail along the river as her guide. If she was lucky, she'd be able to reach Tanner's cabin by nightfall. And if she was really lucky, maybe he'd be home.

"Please be home," she whispered, a strange desperation welling within her—a desperation for someone who would understand and care and want to help. She had no one else now that Nelly was so ill.

The truth was, Tanner had become her closest friend since moving to the area. And even though she only saw him every couple of weeks, their friendship always seemed to pick up right where they'd left off. Even with the five-year gap in age, they had always been able to talk easily, and she loved the way he teased her—as if she were his sister.

She could admit that, at times, she'd felt more than sisterly feelings toward Tanner. It was hard not to when he was so charming and had a lopsided grin that could knock the breath from her lungs.

Confound it all, but he was good-looking enough to win a prize for being Colorado's handsomest man. His features were strong and masculine and always so full of life and energy. He had brown hair the color of a beaver pelt and brown eyes just as rich. His jaw and chin were covered in a perpetual layer of dark scruff, which only added to his ruggedness.

Even though she'd always battled attraction to him, she'd done her best to ignore the fluttering and flopping that went on in her stomach whenever he was around. Because the simple fact was, he'd never shown an interest in her beyond friendship. Even if he had, she wouldn't have been willing to let anything more than friendship develop. He was a mountain man through and through and could never offer her the normal life she longed for.

"Tanner Oakley, you're a good man," she said as she wobbled again and grasped at the rocky bank to steady herself. "But it doesn't matter how good you are; all you'll ever be is my friend."

Regardless, she hoped he'd be home and could help her with Nelly.

Fresh urgency prodded her again. "Hold on, Nelly."

Maisy picked up her pace. If she didn't go faster, Nelly wouldn't survive.

Ahead, Smoke halted, then shifted around, his golden eyes landing upon her warily, as if to warn her.

But before she could assure the wolf that she was fine, her feet slid in the snow, and she careened toward the edge of the path. Before she could grab on to another root, she slipped and fell to her backside.

She flailed and tried to find something to hold, but the ground beneath her was too slick. In the next instant, she was sliding over the embankment into a free fall toward the dark chasm below.

Her heart flew up into her throat, cutting off a scream. She was gonna crash to the rocky bottom a hundred feet below.

Her feet hit something, and her body jolted to an abrupt halt, cushioned by her rucksack. Even so, the impact knocked the wind from her lungs.

She hadn't fallen all the way—must have landed on an outcropping.

She pushed up to get a better view, but her feet again began to slip out from underneath her. Rapidly, she scrambled backward until her back connected with the cliffside. Her fingers latched on to a shrub growing from a crack in the rocks, and she clasped it tightly, fighting against the slippery coating of ice that threatened to pull her toward the abyss and her death below.

As she steadied herself, she gasped for a breath, and her heartbeat echoed loudly in her chest. Was she safe? At the very least, she was alive.

Though shadowed, the faint light of dawn illuminated the area around her, revealing a ledge that was perhaps ten feet long and six feet deep. It wasn't much, but it was something.

She lifted her head and glanced up. Smoke's face was peeking over the trail edge, his eyes riveted to her.

How far had she fallen?

A dozen feet? Two dozen?

It was close enough that she could hear Smoke's whimper.

"I'm okay." At least, she hoped she was. She didn't think she had any broken bones or cuts. Even if she didn't, she'd likely have a few big bruises.

She searched the ledge and then the granite cliffside. It was straight up and down except for the slight slope where she'd first fallen off the path.

Was she stuck?

A sick weight settled in her chest.

There was nothing she could do at the moment. Not with how icy it was.

She would have to wait until it warmed up and then do her best to figure out a way to rescue herself. Because she'd learned she couldn't rely on anyone but herself. If she didn't save herself, not only would Nelly surely die, but so would she.

2

What was he doing with his life?

Tanner Oakley finished resetting the iron foothold trap and lifted his face into the fading afternoon sunshine. After the cold morning, the high-altitude rays felt good on his skin. But his fingers were still stiff, his back sore, and his feet weary.

Was he growing soft after his weeks out East?

He stood and stretched, letting himself take in the grand view of Gold Bend River. It was wide and rocky, with fast-flowing rapids churning up foam and spray. The riverbanks, thick with Douglas fir and ponderosa pine, provided an undisturbed habitat for the sage grouse, blue grouse, and marmots that were plentiful during the autumn months.

Unlike some trappers, who had no regard for the natural cycle of life, he was careful not to kill animals needlessly and only during the proper hunting seasons.

And after the past five years of living in the wilderness, he'd become an expert at hunting and trapping.

But all that experience didn't seem to matter today. Nothing seemed to matter. Not even the majesty of the wilderness all around him.

The question echoed through him again: what was he doing with his life? Especially now that he was done searching for his long-lost family.

The disappointment from his failed mission in New York City swelled again, as it had often during the train ride back to Colorado earlier in the week. He'd gone east with his brother Ryder over six weeks ago, hoping to investigate more into their past, but he'd run into dead ends with every path he'd taken.

Having grown up as an orphan who knew nothing about his birth family, Tanner had long desired to find out more, even after the Oakley family had adopted Ryder and him. In fact, the need had grown so desperate over the past years that he'd thought of little else. Back in January, after his adoptive pa had died, he'd finally hired an investigator with his fur-trapping and trail-guide earnings.

The investigator had narrowed down wagon train parties on the Oregon Trail that had been attacked by Natives, because that was all he and Ryder knew—that they'd been traveling west with their parents, and their wagon train had been attacked by Natives.

Even that knowledge hadn't been entirely certain. It had come secondhand from a pair of cowboys who had delivered him and Ryder to a Chicago orphanage. The two had claimed to have picked them up from a tribe of Kickapoo in Kansas.

No one was sure how long they'd lived with the Kickapoo—probably not too long, according to the cowboys. Maybe a few months. For lack of names or other identifying information, the orphanage workers had named him and Ryder after the cowboys who'd brought them in.

Tanner only had fleeting memories of his parents and the time before the attack—memories of snuggling on a lap or listening to a violin being played. He had vague recollections of a kind man and woman who had both been young and earnest. But he'd only been a toddler— had just turned three.

Ryder, on the other hand, had been five, and Tanner had never been able to understand how his brother couldn't recall a single detail of their lives—not even their names. But for the longest time, Ryder hadn't been able to remember anything.

They hadn't liked the Chicago orphanage. After living there for six months, they'd convinced the staff that they were from New York City and had family there, even though Ryder hadn't known where they were from any more than he'd known their names. But he had suspected they were from the East and not Chicago.

Having been taken to New York by train, they'd then been shuffled from one overcrowded orphanage to the next. Somehow Ryder had managed to keep them from getting separated over the years. Through all the changes and upheaval, Ryder had taken care of Tanner, had been like a parent.

Even so, Tanner had lived with the frustration of not knowing about his past. And during the last year, he'd gotten angry at Ryder for not trying to discover more too. But Ryder hadn't cared, didn't need the resolution in the same way.

Tanner could admit he'd been belligerent toward Ryder about the whole issue. But being the good brother that he was, Ryder had stuck with him and loved him regardless.

Recently, Ryder had a breakthrough, remembering the day of the wagon train attack and recalling some names. He'd only been able to list first names, learning that his given name was Edward and Tanner's was Donny—probably a shortened form of Donald. They thought their mother's name was Sarah and their father's possibly Hawthorne. While the information had been something, it hadn't been enough to make any progress in the investigation. Not without a last name, and that was something Ryder still couldn't remember, maybe never would.

Tanner had finally given up the hope that he'd ever find out who his family really was.

He rubbed a hand against the kink in his back, but no amount of pushing or prodding could get rid of the restless knot that had formed deep inside. Now that he was no longer searching for his family, what would he do?

He'd returned to his cabin along Eagle's Nest Lake yesterday and had planned to resume his life. But he'd been restless all night and now again all day.

He glanced upriver in the direction of the lake and his cabin. Was it time to move on to a new place?

Lots of mountain men grew discontent after a few years in the same area and moved on for the next adventure. Maybe that was what he needed to do. Nothing was tying him down, especially since Ryder was no longer around.

At the crackle of brush along the riverbank trail to the south, his hand slid to the rifle hanging from his shoulder. Someone—or some creature—was coming.

Tanner silently stepped out of sight into the shadows of a fir tree, and in the same move, he readied his rifle.

The footsteps on the path were too soft and the tread too fast for a human. The heaviness was that of a larger creature. Perhaps a deer?

His stomach chose that moment to rumble. He'd brought fresh provisions from town to his cabin, but he hadn't been back all day. And now, with sunset but an hour or so away, maybe he'd be able to shoot a buck and feast on fresh venison.

With a slow peek around the fir tree, he lifted his rifle and aimed down the path.

In the next instant, the creature broke through the low brush and bounded closer. Not a deer, but a small-sized wolf with a gray snout and white-and-gray markings on its body.

"Smoke?" Tanner lowered his rifle.

At the sight of Tanner, the creature halted, panting, its tongue hanging out, and its chest heaving. Familiar gold eyes locked on to Tanner.

"What are you doing here?" Tanner scanned the woodland along the riverbank for any sign of Maisy. Usually, wherever Smoke was, Maisy was close by. The devoted wolf never strayed far from her.

Smoke turned and paced a few feet back on the trail but didn't disappear from sight.

Maisy had been the bright spot in Tanner's mountain-living over the past few years, like starlight in an otherwise dark sky. Even if she was beautiful, with her red hair and blue-green eyes, she'd always been too young for him to think about romantically, and he'd done his best to treat her like a sibling, although he wasn't above flirting and teasing with her.

Through their interactions, he'd grown to admire and respect her independence and intelligence. She was as savvy as a mountain man. She knew the trails well, could hunt any wild game, and foraged better than many Natives. Not only could she survive in the wild, but she was caring and compassionate to people and animals alike.

He searched the trail again. How long had it been? A month? Maybe two?

Although he'd thought about her and Nelly from time to time while he'd been out East, he hadn't worried about them—primarily because he was so confident in Maisy's abilities. She'd proven her wilderness know-how time and time again. And even though her father and Glenn were gone for long periods, she had Nelly to watch over her and keep her out of trouble.

Tanner shouldered his rifle and waited for the first sight of her, his breath catching in his chest with the anticipation of looking at her pretty face and into her stunning eyes.

Smoke was still in the same place, his gaze unwavering upon Tanner. And filled with urgency.

A small alarm began to ring inside Tanner. "Where's Maisy?" He directed his question to Smoke as if the wolf could somehow answer him.

The creature just started down the trail, this time disappearing into the brush.

"Maisy?" Tanner called. He waited several heartbeats for her reply, but when it didn't come, the alarm inside grew louder.

He took several steps down the path but then stopped. Smoke might just be out hunting, as he did from time to time. That didn't necessarily mean something had happened to Maisy. He couldn't let his thoughts immediately jump to the worst conclusions.

But then again, Smoke had never come directly to him without Maisy before. And the creature had never been so winded or so anxious.

Maybe he should head out to the Merritts' place for a visit. He'd been planning to do so soon—in a couple of days, after he'd had the chance to set his traps and settle back in.

Tanner glanced through the branches to the sky, which was changing to a darker blue as evening drew near. There wasn't enough daylight left for him to make the trek to Arapahoe Valley. He'd have to head back to his cabin tonight and leave in the morning.

He turned and started toward where he'd tied his gelding.

A yipping from down the trail echoed in the air. It was Smoke. Was there an urgency to the wolf's barking?

Tanner halted. What if Smoke had come for him because something had happened to either Maisy or Nelly?

How could he ignore the wolf?

Tanner hesitated only a moment longer before continuing on his way to his horse, anxiety lengthening each step. His spotted Oakley was waiting right where he'd tethered it. Tanner wasted no time in mounting and starting downriver. It only took him half a minute to come upon Smoke, standing in the center of the trail and facing him with an impatient look—if that were possible for a wolf.

At Tanner's approach, Smoke bounded forward into a run and disappeared again down the trail. Tanner knew he'd never be able to keep up. His mount was used to the rough terrain, but wolves were naturally nimble and could outrace most other mountain animals.

Regardless, Tanner pushed his gelding hard, his own urgency growing with each passing mile. When the sun disappeared behind the peaks and darkness crowded in, he finally had to slow down. Even then, however, he kept a steady pace, having trekked the mountain trails often enough in the dark to be able to navigate, especially because he had some moonlight to guide the way when he wasn't in the thick of the woods.

Smoke stayed well ahead, halting once in a while to wait for Tanner to catch up before bounding ahead. When they finally reached Arapahoe Gully, Smoke began to lead him up the sharp trail that led to the Merritt cabin. It was in a beautiful area overlooking Gold Bend River and the valley, but in Tanner's opinion, Cleveland Merritt had been a fool to build on the hillside rather than down in the river valley where the land was level for growing crops and plentiful with water.

But Cleveland wasn't usually one to stop and think about anyone but himself. He was a decent fellow with good morals—at least, for a mountain man. But Tanner didn't like that he dragged his womenfolk all around into such wild and untamed areas. Not only did it make life harder for them, but they were isolated and away from civilization.

Tanner dismounted and led his horse for the climb up the trail to the house. By the time he made the last turn, he passed Smoke. The creature had finally stopped and was sitting, his breathing heavy and his exhaustion palpable.

The wolf had brought him here. That had become clear enough during the past hours.

As Tanner nudged his horse up the last incline, he took in the position of the moon and tried to gauge the passing of time. He guessed he'd been riding hard for six or seven hours, and it was likely past midnight.

In the clearing ahead, the outline of the cabin came into view, even though it was shrouded in darkness by the tall pines that hovered around it. It was bigger than his own place, but not by much. And it was completely dark, without a sliver of light anywhere. But that was normal for the late hour. Why would the women use up precious oil or coal when they were slumbering?

He scanned the area, including the stable and shed

behind the cabin, searching for anything unusual. He could make out pelts bundled in neat stacks under the overhang, along with horse feed and cut wood. Traps and rope dangled from the ceiling beams. A sack of chicken feed sat near a watering trough.

Everything appeared just as orderly as when he'd ridden away after his last visit in August.

But the horses were gone, which meant Cleveland and Glenn weren't home.

As Tanner halted just outside the cabin, he hesitated. Had he been foolish to follow the wolf? What if he knocked on the door only to wake up Maisy and Nelly?

Rather than disturb them, maybe he ought to bed down in the stable for the night.

Tanner sighed. He'd hurried all this way thinking something was wrong, and now he needed to reassure himself that all was well.

He approached the door and rapped the wood softly. If he got lucky, maybe he'd only wake Nelly.

She'd been expecting a baby when he left. Maybe she'd given birth to the child by now.

He waited, but the silence was eerie.

After several more seconds, he knocked again, this time louder. He pressed his ear to the door, but he still couldn't hear any movement inside.

A scolding squeak from a nearby tree startled him.

He had his revolver out before he realized it and

before he saw the glint of eyes staring down at him from the barren limb of a dead fir tree next to the stable.

"Roscoe?" he whispered.

The creature replied with another squeak, as if to confirm his identity.

Why wasn't Nelly answering the door?

The strange unease he'd been feeling for the past hours came rushing back. He knocked again, pounding loudly enough to awaken anyone slumbering inside.

He waited only a few seconds before opening the door.

Darkness greeted him, and a chill hung in the air, the stove unlit.

"Hello?" he called, abandoning the idea of not waking anyone up. "Maisy, Nelly?"

More silence greeted him.

Was no one home?

He crossed to where he knew the table sat, then fumbled in the dark, locating the lantern that was usually at the center. It took him a moment to light it, but once the flame was going, he lifted the lantern and glanced around.

At the form of a body in the bed, he jolted forward, his heart racing with dread. Maisy. What if something had happened to her?

As he reached the bedside, the light spilled over Nelly's pale face. It wasn't Maisy.

But what if it had been?

He'd taken for granted that she'd be okay here, that she was strong enough to survive. But what if he'd been wrong?

He placed the lantern on the barrel that served as a bedside table, then hovered his fingers above Nelly's lips, hoping to feel breath. But there was nothing. He moved his fingers to her neck, trying to find a pulse, but she was clearly gone. Her body was thin and her stomach flat, which meant she'd had her baby.

He scanned the cabin but could find no sign of the infant—no tiny clothing, no drying diapers, no little blankets.

The newborn must have died, and now Nelly had died too, possibly recently.

His pulse began to tap hard with understanding. Maisy had probably gone after help. That's why she wasn't here. But why hadn't she stopped by his place? Maybe she had and he hadn't been back yet. Or maybe she'd been in too much of a hurry to get to town and hadn't taken the time to visit.

No, with the situation so grave, she would have sought him out and asked to borrow his horse for the remainder of the trip into Breckenridge. So why hadn't she? And Smoke. The wolf would have stayed with her the whole trip. And he hadn't.

Tanner stalked back to the open door and peered

around the dark yard. There was no sign of her anywhere. He spun and took in the cabin—the same as always, nothing out of the ordinary . . . except for Nelly's lifeless body.

There was no other explanation for Maisy's absence except that she'd gotten into trouble of some kind.

He palmed the back of his neck, the tension in his body coiling tighter with each passing moment. A dozen scenarios clamored through his head, each one horrible. What if she'd gotten caught in a trap? Or mauled by a wild animal? Or attacked by a thief?

He dropped his hand and slapped the doorpost in frustration. Why in the blazes had Cleveland left the women here alone? Why would any sane man leave women to fend for themselves? It wasn't right. If Cleveland wanted to be a mountain man, he shouldn't have gotten married and had children.

That's why Tanner hadn't settled down with a woman yet. Because his wandering lifestyle wasn't right for a wife and family. At least he had the good sense to see the truth and live by it.

Regardless, he had to find Maisy. He'd honed his tracking skills over the years, and never had he been gladder to know how to track than right now.

A wolf's yipping echoed from a distance. Was Smoke still back on the trail? Was the wolf trying to lead him to Maisy?

A shiver raced up Tanner's spine. Yes, Smoke had been guiding him the whole time and still was. Tanner could only pray he wasn't too late.

At Smoke's yipping from the trail above, Maisy bolted awake.

Immediately her teeth started chattering, the cold temperature of the night having penetrated through the layers of her coat and clothing. After sitting on the ledge all day with a cold October breeze hitting her, she'd already been chilled to the bone when darkness had fallen hours ago.

But after nightfall and the steady drop in the temperature, she'd grown even more miserable, her limbs stiff, her toes and fingers numb, her face raw. She'd tried to stay awake, knowing she needed to continue to generate warmth in her body throughout the long night. But at the late hour, exhaustion had made her sluggish, and she'd finally decided to rest for an hour or two.

Another wolf yip sounded in the air. Smoke had lingered on the trail after she'd fallen onto the ledge and had watched her for long hours as she'd attempted to scale the cliff wall, searching for hand and footholds. But no matter how many times she'd tried to hoist herself up, she'd always slipped back down. The cliff was too steep and the ledge too far down.

When she'd finally admitted defeat and lowered herself to the ground, Smoke had disappeared and had been gone ever since. She'd hoped and prayed that he was seeking help in some way—although she wasn't sure how. And now he was back.

She tried to push herself up, but painful prickles in her arms and legs stopped her.

"Smoke?" The word was hoarse.

A softer bark replied.

She lifted her head and peered up through the darkness. Moonlight illuminated Smoke's head peeking over the side, his eyes glowing. She'd hoped to see a neighbor with him, maybe even her pa. But the wolf was alone.

Her heart thudded a slow beat of despair. Without the help, she wasn't going anywhere.

"Thanks for trying," she croaked to the wolf.

Smoke lifted his head and stared up the trail before turning back to her and whining.

She wasn't sure she'd be able to survive the night, especially since the temperature had gone down even more over the past hour. The truth was, she had to get up and keep moving—as much as she could on the ledge.

If she could make it through the night, she'd buy more time. Maybe Smoke would be able to find help tomorrow. Or maybe someone would come by.

Once again, Smoke raised his head and barked, this time without stopping.

Was that the wolf's plan, to bark the rest of the night? She wasn't sure what good that would do. Lester Acker was two miles away, and it would take a miracle for him to hear the noise.

"I'm coming." A voice called from somewhere on the trail. A man's voice.

"Help!" Her pulse leapt, and this time she pushed herself up to her feet in spite of the pain. "Help me, please!"

Smoke stopped his yipping.

"Maisy?" The voice grew louder and sounded like Tanner's.

"I'm here!"

In the next instant, lantern light glowed on the trail above, and Tanner was crouching beside Smoke, his keen eyes taking in her predicament. He was wearing his usual coonskin cap, buckskin jacket with shoulder fringes, and thick leather gloves. "You injured?"

"Nope, just a few scrapes and bruises." Thankfully, that was all. "And I'm cold enough to put goose bumps on a burning log."

He scanned the ledge and then the cliffside. "I'll have to fetch a rope."

She nodded. "It's the only way."

He took her in, his face etched with worry lines. His cheeks and jaw were more angular than she remembered, the layer of scruff darker. His hair was cropped neatly—shorter than normal—and his brows furrowed above his rounded eyes.

She stared right back at him, relief mingling with something she couldn't name. She only knew that she loved seeing him there on the trail, loved knowing he'd been willing to follow Smoke, loved that he'd cared enough to come.

With a final scan of her face, he began to back away from the edge. "I'll be right back." He disappeared, taking the light with him, leaving her in darkness again with Smoke standing guard above her.

Her heart tapped out her relief. Tanner was here. She would be safe now.

In no time at all, he was back, kneeling above her and lowering a rope that he'd looped. "How long have you been stuck?"

She gave him the short version of everything that had happened as she hoisted her rucksack to her back and then climbed as he simultaneously tugged her upward.

When she was near the top, he reached down and latched on to her arm. "You're fortunate you landed on the ledge and didn't keep falling."

"You don't have to tell me that." She'd counted her blessings numerous times throughout the day. She'd been reminding herself that, even though she was stuck, the situation could've been much worse.

His frown held censure. "You should have known better than to head out on slick trails."

"All I could think about was getting Nelly help." She'd been foolish and tired and worried. And he was right. She should have waited. Little good she'd done her sister, trapped on the ledge all day.

With one of his hands hauling her up with the rope and the other now gripping her body, he pulled her the rest of the distance—which was fine with her since she was cold and weak and didn't have much energy left.

He dragged her over the cliffside, away from the drop. Before she knew what he was doing, he was hefting her onto his lap and wrapping his arms around her in a hug.

She didn't quite know what to make of the hug and didn't move for several seconds. But as he tightened his hold, she let herself relax against him and embraced him.

"Thank the good Lord you're safe," he murmured, burying his face in the crook of her neck.

His nose and his warm breath caressed her bare skin. They'd never had any physical contact before except briefly in passing. The sensation of his touch and his closeness was different and new.

Now every part of her body was flush against every part of his—or at least, it seemed that way. Her backside was pressed against his hard thighs, her face burrowed into his broad chest, and her hands gripped his taut back.

The feel of him wasn't unpleasant. In fact, it was comforting, as if she'd finally reached a solid and safe place. A part of her mind tried to remind her that Tanner was neither solid nor safe. He was a mountain man like her pa and was everything she didn't want in a man.

But for the moment, she thrust aside the warning and simply rested against him, basking in his comfort. In spite of his body heat, she was still much too cold, and at a gust of wind blowing against her, she shuddered.

He lifted his head so that he was gazing at her, their faces only inches apart. The lantern on the ground beside him cast enough light over his face that she could see every handsome detail of his features. And somehow, after the weeks of not seeing him, he seemed different. Older, perhaps. Sadder. More serious.

The dark brown of his eyes radiated worry. "You're freezing."

She didn't want to move from their position, was afraid that once he released her, he'd never hold her again like this. So she gripped the back of his coat, digging her fingers into the soft leather. "I'm okay now."

He shook his head. "Let's get you inside and warmed up."

She breathed in his outdoorsy scent—a mixture of pine and woodsmoke. Then she gave herself a mental shake. What was she doing, acting like an infatuated girl around him, letting her head be turned so easily?

With a huff, she released him and started to stand. Before she could get too far, he rose and scooped her off her feet in one motion. As he straightened, he held her in both arms and cradled her against his chest—an expanse of chest that rivaled the wide, mountain peaks that rose above them.

"I can walk, Tanner." Her protest was feeble at best.

"I know." He started forward. "But I want to help."

She didn't struggle to free herself. Instead, she latched her arms around his neck, once again unable to contain the thrill of feeling his body against hers.

For as much as she liked the charming and flirtatious Tanner who could make her smile and laugh and forget about her worries, she liked this mature and concerned Tanner even better. Maybe because men usually didn't show all that much concern over her well-being. Maybe because most of the time she had to be strong enough on her own. Maybe because she wanted someone she could lean on once in a while.

He climbed back up the hill effortlessly, managing to balance her and the lantern. Smoke raced ahead, stopping near Tanner's horse, which thankfully was used to seeing the wolf and didn't react.

The cabin was dark and the door ajar. And even though she didn't want to think about anyone or anything except for Tanner and how much she liked being in his arms, the responsibility of caring for Nelly raced back to confront her.

"Can I borrow your horse, Tanner?" She pulled back enough that she could gaze upon his face and gauge his expression. "I need to leave. Now. And go after the doctor for Nelly."

He didn't respond and his footsteps didn't waver as he continued toward the cabin. The only reaction she could see was a twitch in his upper lip—a very handsome upper lip, if she did say so herself. It was strong but slightly curled in a way that hinted at his easy smile.

But at the moment, he offered her no smile. His brows only slanted into a frown.

"I know what you're gonna say," she continued hurriedly. "That I should wait till the morning. But I can't. She's so sick and needs the help quick-like."

He bumped the door wide and stepped inside. The lantern illuminated the cluttered room, unchanged from the way she'd left it earlier in the day, including Nelly, who still lay motionless on the bed.

"Maisy," Tanner started in a serious tone.

"Please don't start acting all protective, big guy." It would be dangerous to travel during the night, which was why she'd waited until dawn to leave. But with the bright moon out, she'd at least have some light for the journey. And if she went by horse, she'd have a much easier time than traveling by foot.

"Listen." Smoke crept into the cabin, and Tanner toed the door closed behind the creature. "If anyone was going back out tonight, it would be me—"

"That's not fair."

"You could have died out there, Maisy." His tone was laced with frustration.

"But I didn't."

He moved toward the table and placed the lantern down. She could feel him getting ready to set her back on her feet, so she clung to his neck. She wasn't sure why she didn't want to let go yet, but she didn't.

He seemed to drag in a deep breath, as though bracing himself. Then he spoke in a rush. "Neither of us needs to go out for the doctor, because Nelly died."

Maisy's heartbeat halted, and her gaze swung to the bed and to Nelly's pale face. Nelly hadn't made it. "Are you sure?" Maisy wriggled to free herself, needing to go to her sister to test the truth for herself.

This time Tanner clung to her. "I'm positive. I came to the cabin first, and she was gone."

At the gravity of his tone, Maisy ceased struggling, closed her eyes, and held back the rush of heated tears. Although she'd known Nelly had given up the will to live and would likely die, the loss still hit with a blow of overwhelming grief.

"I'm sorry, darlin'." Tanner's words were soft and filled with compassion.

The sting of tears only burned hotter, and she couldn't hold them back. They squeezed out and ran down her cheeks. When she pushed against Tanner again, he set her on her feet but held on to her arms for a moment longer than necessary, as though he wanted to comfort her but didn't quite know how.

She had the strange need to fall against him and seek his comfort somehow, but she forced herself to break away and cross to the bed and her sister's body. She laid a hand against Nelly's cheek, and the cold pallor told her that the life had been gone a while, maybe all day.

Maisy wanted to blame herself. If only she'd left a few days ago. If only she'd known how to doctor Nelly herself. If only she'd been able to figure out a way to encourage Nelly not to give up. And maybe all of it was true. Maybe she could've done more.

Even as guilt rose swiftly inside her, she let the simmering resentment toward her pa and Glenn bubble up. They were ultimately at fault. They should have returned earlier, especially since they knew Nelly had had a previous stillbirth that had been hard on her. The two should have realized the potential for problems this time and made a point of being around close to the birthing.

Maisy caressed her sister's cheek. Nelly had always had such a sweet spirit and gentle smile. She'd been generous and kind and loving, had taken care of Maisy and looked after her every need for so many years. Maisy couldn't have asked for a better sister.

Course, she hadn't agreed with all of Nelly's decisions, particularly her choice to marry Glenn and follow in their ma's footsteps. She'd encouraged Nelly to find a different man, one who could give her a better life. But Nelly had married Glenn regardless of Maisy's pleading.

If only Nelly had listened . . .

Maisy swallowed the regrets and the bitterness. It wouldn't do any good to think about what could've been. All she could do was learn from her sister's mistakes and not repeat them for herself.

At the brush of an arm against hers, she sensed Tanner's desire to be there for her during this hard time. He was a steadfast friend to have come all the way to the cabin with Smoke. And he was a steadfast friend to stand by her side now.

She took off her Stetson and tossed it onto the end of the bed, then let her body sag against him.

He slipped his arm around her back and braced her up as though lending her his strength. She wasn't so proud and independent that she would refuse his offer.

For long moments, she stood there against him, watching Nelly, letting the tears fall and silently grieving the loss of so beautiful a woman.

"If Pa hadn't dragged us out here with him," Maisy whispered, "it might not have ended this way."

"I agree," Tanner whispered in response.

"Really?" She swiped the tears from her cheeks.

Tanner stared down at Nelly, his jaw rigid. "In my opinion, mountain men who get married are only thinking about their own needs and not what's best for their wife and children."

"Those are my thoughts exactly. But I didn't realize you felt the same way."

He cast her a sideways glance before focusing back on Nelly. "Why do you think I'm still single?"

"I always thought it was because no woman could put up with how ornery you are." Even in the midst of the grief of losing Nelly, she couldn't overlook a chance to tease Tanner.

His upper lip quirked into half a grin. "That too."

She bumped her shoulder against his arm. "Sometimes I've wondered if I'm crazy for feeling the way I do about this life, about being left behind so often by the menfolk."

He gently bumped her back. "No, you're not crazy. It's not fair of your pa to come and go as he pleases, leaving you responsible for so much while he's away for such long stretches."

The affirmation brought tears to her eyes again, and she had to blink rapidly to keep them from spilling over.

"Ever since I turned eighteen, Pa's been talking about having me marry one of his partners up in Wyoming."

Tanner stiffened. "He's never said anything to me about that."

"I told him I'd rather throw myself off the edge of a cliff."

"Oh, so that's what you did this morning?" Tanner's voice held the familiar note of teasing that she loved so much.

"Yep, you figured me out."

"I'm sure Cleveland wasn't too happy about you telling him no."

That was an understatement. Her pa had ranted on and on at her declaration. "He can't understand why I want a normal life with a normal husband. Nelly didn't understand either."

"I understand. Don't let him pressure you into something you don't want."

"I won't. I'm holding out for a pretty house in town—one with two stories and painted shutters, a front porch with a swing, and a fenced-in backyard with bird feeders and space to take care of all the baby animals that need nurturing."

Tanner's arm brushed against hers, and she liked the feel of him by her side. She liked it a lot. And she was glad she didn't have to face Nelly's death alone.

Tanner wanted to punch something. Preferably Cleveland Merritt's face for abandoning his daughters in the wilderness.

Because of his recklessness, Nelly was dead. And Maisy could have died today—maybe would have frozen to death on the ledge if he hadn't come along.

"Thanks for coming," she said, as if reading his mind.

"I'm just glad Smoke found me."

From their spot beside the bed, she was leaning into him, and he had the urge to slip his arm around her. Just to lend his support. Not because he wanted to feel her body against his again.

No, now wasn't the time to think about how good she'd felt when he'd held her on the path or when he'd carried her up to the cabin. In fact, there would never be a time to think about how good she'd felt.

He couldn't let his mind drift that direction. She was

off-limits. Completely and totally off-limits. She always had been and always would be.

She rested her head against his arm, her petite height hardly reaching his shoulder. Without her hat holding her hair up, waves fell over her shoulders, cascading nearly to her waist. The lantern light turned the red to fiery flames—flames that seemed to flicker and dance and taunt him to reach out and touch them.

An inner voice scolded him against touching, reminding him that flames were hot and he didn't want to get burned. Worse, he didn't want Maisy to get hurt because of his carelessness.

So far in his short life, he'd never been careless or casual in his relationships with women—not the way his brother had been. Sure, he'd flirted, had fun with women, and had even exchanged a few kisses that had been offered to him. But he'd always known where to draw the line and had never crossed it, had prided himself on his self-control.

He intended to use every ounce of self-control he possessed with Maisy now too, just as he always had.

The problem was, he'd never held her before. And now that he had, his body was suddenly attuned to every little thing about her.

She shifted and lifted her hand into the crook of his arm, settling her fingers there as naturally as if she did it every day.

Except it wasn't natural for him. It only made his entire body alert to her fingers circling his bicep.

He wanted to lift his hand and cover hers. Maybe he'd even graze his thumb across the back of her hand. The need was swift and forceful, and he swallowed against it, balling his fists and stiffening his arm.

"Now that Nelly's gone," she said softly, "I've got no reason to stay here."

Yes, he needed to get his mind off her touch and onto a different subject. "What will you do?"

She shrugged and the movement accentuated the way her bosom was brushing his arm—her generous bosom.

His mouth went dry. When had she grown up so fully? Of course, he'd noticed her changing into a woman over the past couple of years. It would have been hard not to see just how lovely she was. With every visit, she'd only seemed to grow more beautiful.

Maybe that was his problem tonight. After the past weeks away from her, she'd matured even more. And it was easy to see that all traces of the girl she'd once been were gone and that she was all grown up now.

Maisy released a soft sigh, and even that small breath seemed to knock into him and send his senses into a rush of strange need.

"My ma has family back in Minnesota. She always spoke fondly of a sister. Maybe I can write to her and see if she'll let me live with her, just till I can find work."

"What kind of work?" He could only think of one type of work available to women, and he'd never let Maisy get so desperate that she'd have to resort to it.

"Decent work, Tanner." She pushed against him, clearly hearing the hesitancy in his tone. "I've got lots of talent. You've said so yourself."

"Talent at surviving in the wilderness. And taking in wild critters who need mothering. But I doubt you'll find any work doing that in Minnesota."

She was silent for a moment, hopefully thinking twice about rushing off and trying to make it on her own. "Reckon if I can't find work there, I'll find myself a husband."

"A husband?" That was an even worse prospect. "You won't know anyone. And you can't travel all that way to end up marrying a stranger."

"Why not?" She lifted one of her shoulders in a shrug. "People answer advertisements and get married for convenience all the time."

He couldn't argue with her there. That's what Ryder had recently done in order to find a mother for his baby. "Still, you deserve more than that. You deserve a man who will cherish and love you."

"Oh, hush up." She laughed lightly. "That's the stuff of fairy tales, and you know it. I'll be happy if I can have a man who doesn't leave me every chance he has for months on end."

Tanner's gut was tightening with each passing second of their conversation, the same way it had tightened when she'd said Cleveland was pressuring her about marrying a partner in Wyoming.

Maisy was someone special. He'd noticed it the first time he'd met her a few years ago. He'd stopped by to introduce himself to Cleveland and offer a hand as they built their cabin, and she'd come running out of the woods in bare feet, her skirt hiked into trousers underneath and her hair unbound and blowing like wildfire. She'd been cradling a sickly and injured baby eagle that had likely been abandoned and left to die, and she'd been determined to nurse it back to health.

She'd been so full of life and passion that he'd been left speechless.

As much as he'd been enamored by Maisy and her sass and liveliness, he'd never had the level of awareness that he was having tonight. He could only blame the physical contact he'd inadvertently had with her for stirring up latent desires.

Or maybe his desires had already been awakened because he'd been watching his siblings fall in love over the past year. First his adoptive brother Maverick had gotten married to his childhood sweetheart. Then his adoptive sister Clarabelle had found the love of her life in a German nobleman. And just recently, Ryder had fallen deeply in love with his wife, an heiress from New York City.

With each of his siblings so enamored of their spouses, Tanner had been surrounded by their joy in each other, which included all kinds of physical displays of affection and lots of kissing—lots and lots of it.

Then, after Tanner had returned from the East, Maverick had been excited to share the news that he and Hazel were expecting a baby. Maybe their marriages and the news of the baby had stirred something in him for more . . .

Or maybe now that he'd put to rest his investigation of his family's origins, he was starting to consider his own future and what that would entail. While he'd never thought he'd get married or have children as a mountain man, what if the desire was buried someplace inside?

Maybe he'd let his past—or lack of a past—dictate his life for too long. All his energy and passion had centered on finding his family. And now that he was done looking, he needed to move on and do something meaningful with his life. The trouble was, he didn't really know what that was.

Whatever was contributing to his heightened awareness of Maisy tonight, he had to let it go and continue on with their relationship the way it had always been. He hadn't ever considered dallying with her before, and just because they were alone and unchaperoned right now didn't mean he'd give himself permission to start.

Maisy's thumb rubbed his bicep again, and every

nerve in his body sparked to life. The trouble was, she was so innocent and always had been. She didn't realize how attractive she was. And she certainly wasn't aware of how her touch was affecting him now that she was an adult.

He had to take a step away from her, had to break the spell she was casting over him—one that made him much too aware of how desirable she was.

The trouble was, he had no right to see her as desirable. None at all.

With a force of will from deep inside, he broke away from her and crossed back to the table. He stood facing it and palmed the back of his neck. Normally he wasn't so tongue-tied, but this new tension he was feeling with her was confusing him.

"Reckon I oughta get her ready for her burying." Maisy's voice was soft and sad.

He glanced at her over his shoulder to find the tears rolling down her cheeks again as she clutched Nelly's hand.

He stifled a curse at himself. He was being a selfish cad, thinking about how attractive she was at a time like this. What was wrong with him?

He shook his head sternly at his own callousness. Then he headed for the bucket near the door. "I'll get some fresh water so you can heat it and give her a bath."

"Thank you, Tanner."

He didn't say more as he stepped outside. Instead, he

closed the door behind himself and paused on the hard dirt path that had been worn away in front of the cabin. He drew in a deep breath of night air and let the coolness soothe his overheated skin.

He'd clearly been too long without feminine companionship. Maybe next time he was back at his adopted family's ranch near Breckenridge, he'd have to head into town and join in a social event. Sometimes there were dances or parties or picnics. If he spent more time with other women, maybe he wouldn't act like a bull in heat around Maisy.

For a short while, he busied himself fetching water from a nearby mountain stream—one that was as clear and clean as well water. When he returned to the cabin, Maisy had already set out Nelly's best outfit. He stoked the fire, set the water to boil, and then offered to build a simple coffin with the boards he knew were stored in the stable. So while Maisy bathed and dressed Nelly, he retreated to the stable to give them the privacy they deserved, then set to work there, cutting the boards and nailing them together.

By the time they'd both finished, dawn was beginning to lighten the sky. They laid Nelly in the coffin, and Maisy took her time fixing her sister's hair and making her look pretty. Finally, they carried the coffin to the small graveyard containing the stone marker of Nelly's first stillborn baby and now the fresh grave from her second.

Tanner began digging, and Maisy found a second shovel and joined in. When they had a sufficient and deep enough hole, they laid Nelly to rest. Tanner said a few words first, then Maisy ended with a heartfelt prayer. Smoke stood beside them, and Roscoe came out of his fir tree to chatter at them as if offering a blessing of his own.

By the time they'd finished covering the coffin with earth and pounding it down, the morning sunshine was breaking through the pine branches and giving them light and some warmth. Maisy wanted to find a stone to mark the gravesite, so they searched the perimeter of the cleared land for something that would work.

When Maisy was finally happy with the stone she'd selected, Tanner worked at carving Nelly's name and lifespan into the rock. While he did that, Maisy cut several berry branches and pine boughs and formed a wreath.

As she stepped back from placing the wreath next to the headstone, she swiped at her cheeks, leaving a streak of dirt amidst the tears. Her eyes were red-rimmed, her face splotchy, and her nose sniffling, and his heart welled with compassion for her.

She'd lost so much—her ma, her sister, and the babies. Now here she was, in her mountain home, all alone.

He'd been peering at the trail to the north and the river bottoms to the south all morning, hoping for a sign of Cleveland and Glenn. But he knew as well as Maisy did that there was no predicting when the two would show up. It could be in a few hours, a few days, or even a few weeks.

Tanner suspected they would be wrapping up their transactions soon. He'd heard they'd been hired on by a group of geologists to guide them through the rough terrain and also to hunt for them. They'd be back in time to do the best fur trapping, which was during the winter months when the animal coats were at their thickest.

The tears continued down Maisy's cheeks. "Goodbye, Nelly. I'll miss you."

The ache inside Tanner's chest swelled. And though he'd kept from touching her since leaving the cabin last night, he couldn't stop himself from touching her in this moment. His hand seemed to have a will of its own, and in the next instant, he took hold of her hand and squeezed it, trying to offer her a measure of solace. He'd just squeeze and let go.

She grasped him back, her fingers trembling.

How could he pull away now? He couldn't. Not when she was in such obvious distress. Instead, he enveloped her hand deeper into his. As he did so, he could feel a shudder work its way through her body, ending on a soft sob.

"Ah, darlin'." He shifted her around and pulled her into an embrace.

She came willingly, falling against him and burying her face into his chest. The sobs came more forcefully.

He tucked her head underneath his chin and wrapped his arms around her fully. And for long minutes he stood with her like that, just letting her cry and rubbing her back gently. The sobs grew softer and disappeared, and eventually she seemed to relax against him.

When she finally exhaled a deep breath, he guessed that was his cue that she was all right, that he needed to release her and step back.

But who could find fault with him for holding her a moment longer in her hour of need? He was comforting her. That's all. And today of all days, that's what she needed. Nothing more.

He rested his chin on her head while he lightly traced her spine up, then down. She had such a graceful curve to her back. And she had such generous curves pressing against his chest.

Blast.

He was doing it again. Being selfish. Thinking of his own needs and desires.

He pulled back.

Before he could step away, she grabbed his flannel shirt into a fist and held him in place. Her tear- and dirt-streaked face was so beautiful. And now, her mesmerizing blue-green eyes peered up at him, so full of questions. She was likely wondering what his embrace meant, and he needed to end it now before she read more into it.

But before he could force himself to let go, her gaze snagged upon his lips—his upper lip—and her pupils widened, darkening her eyes. Was it desire? Was she feeling something for him the same way he was for her?

His pulse leapt to life like a flame fanned by a gust of wind, and heat began to burn in his veins.

5

Tanner's mouth was perfection, especially that curling upper lip.

Maisy had ever only been kissed once, by a young man she'd met in town at a dance shortly after she'd moved to the area. At the time, she'd been curious about kissing and how it would feel, since she'd witnessed Nelly kissing Glenn.

So when the young man—whose name she didn't remember—had walked her out of the Inman's Lodge and dipped his head down for a kiss, she hadn't resisted.

But she certainly hadn't thought it anything special. It had been sloppy and wet. She'd broken it off and walked away, even though the fella had called after her.

In spite of her dismal kissing experience, there was something about Tanner's mouth that told her kissing him would be different. And she wanted to find out how different.

As curious as always, she stood up on her toes, cupped Tanner's face, and in the same motion, brought it down to hers. She touched her lips to his, softly, tentatively, wanting to feel him and test out his appealing lips for herself.

He stood frozen in place, clearly taken by surprise. He didn't back away, but neither did he respond.

And she wanted him to. She wanted him to be interested in kissing her too.

But he'd always treated her with the utmost respect. Even if he was good at flirting, that's all it had ever been—plain and simple flirting and nothing more. He'd never hinted at being attracted to her or wanting anything from her. But last night and today, he'd held her in a way he never had before. That had to mean something, didn't it?

Regardless, she wanted to kiss him. And when she wanted something, she rarely denied herself.

She pressed her lips against his more firmly and with more demand.

His eyes rounded, and he drew in a breath, as though he hadn't expected her to really kiss him. But then he pressed back with a short, sweet peck before pulling away.

Surely a man like Tanner had more to his kisses than soft, sweet pecks.

She aimed to find out. Before he could move too far from her, she slid her hands to the back of his neck and tugged him back down. At the same time, she met his mouth and focused on his upper lip. She teased it with a nibble before taking it more fully and suckling it.

His hand against her spine tightened, and he released a soft growl. In the next instant, his mouth covered hers. Although, *cover* didn't quite describe his move. It was more like he took possession of her mouth, as if he'd paid for it in gold and now it belonged to him.

The surge of his lips was no longer soft or sweet. Instead it was strong and sharp. And this time she was the one to draw in a surprised breath.

Her intake only seemed to fuel his kiss, and he possessed her more deeply, his lips colliding with hers, giving her no choice but to collide back.

Her lashes fluttered closed with the pure pleasure that coursed through her. Yes, this was what she'd wanted to experience with him. Maybe this was what she'd even secretly dreamed of doing with him.

Course, she'd always denied any desire for him beyond friendship. As handsome and charming and sweet as he'd always been, she'd known she had to keep an attraction from forming. What if it had been growing regardless of her efforts to fight against it?

The rhythm of his lips kept pace with hers, and the kiss seemed to take her high into the universe, where she was lost in the vastness of space. But she was lost with him, with just the two of them, spinning and circling until she was dizzy and could hardly stand without crumpling.

She clung to him and wasn't sure how long the colliding kiss lasted—maybe just a few seconds, maybe a minute. Whatever the case, it left her completely breathless, and she had to pull back to gasp for air. At the same time, his labored exhalations taunted her lips, as though to beckon her to let him possess her again.

Oh, dear heavens. The kiss she'd had outside the lodge couldn't begin to compare with Tanner's kiss. It wasn't even close.

In fact, nothing else that she'd previously experienced in life could compare with his kiss. It wasn't real, was it? What if it was just a fluke? What if the next kiss was boring? What if it didn't affect her as much?

He'd seemed to like it and be affected by it. At the very least, he hadn't pushed her away. Instead, his hand on her spine was taut, his fingers pressing into her with a force that radiated all the way to a place deep inside.

She could kiss him again to test things out.

With a shake of his head, almost as if he was frustrated with himself, he began to step away. Before he could break their connection, she tightened her hold around his neck and drew him back, this time more powerfully, surging upward and letting her lips meet with his again.

She wasn't tentative or uncertain about the kissing

any longer. She'd experienced the power of the connection, and she craved more. In fact, every single inch of her body craved another kiss, as though she was starved for it and would die without it.

As her mouth tangled with his, he hesitated but a moment. Then he released another low growl at the back of his throat before joining in the kiss again just as passionately as the last time, perhaps even more so—as if he'd abandoned any need to hold himself back and was giving in to whatever this was that was happening between them.

What exactly was happening?

She didn't understand it. But she wouldn't let that stop her from enjoying this moment with him. Because not only did she love the pressure of their lips fusing, but she loved the pressure of their bodies together. He was so strong and powerful and rugged. And there was something that made her feel secure within the shelter of his arms—so much so that she had a sudden need to stay there with him, be with him, and never leave him. The need flooded her so powerfully she trembled. And she hesitated.

What was she doing kissing Tanner and letting her desires surface like this? She couldn't stay with him, be with him, and never leave him. Not when she'd vowed that she wouldn't become like her ma or Nelly and marry a mountain man.

Their lives had been miserable and lonely and full of heartache. And look how both had ended . . . abandoned by their husbands, without loyalty, without devotion, and without commitment.

As if sensing her hesitation, Tanner broke the kiss and stepped back.

This time, she didn't hold on to him. She let go of him and hugged her arms to her chest.

"Lord in heaven above." Tanner spun and paced to the stable. He stopped abruptly and stood stiffly.

Was he wishing he hadn't kissed her?

She could honestly say that she didn't regret it, that she was glad they'd kissed, that she'd loved every moment of it. But she could also see that doing so might be dangerous. The pleasure from the connection was swirling low inside her belly. Her lips were still warm from the heated kissing, her body still flushed from the contact. It would be all too easy to throw herself upon him again and keep kissing and holding him without stopping . . .

Her mind flashed to the times when Glenn had been home and had shared the bed with Nelly.

Embarrassed heat speared her cheeks. From her pallet on the floor, she'd always tried to sleep and ignore the two, doing her best to give them some privacy. But she wasn't naïve. She knew where all the kissing and hugging eventually led. And that end had to be reserved for the marriage bed.

And since marriage to Tanner was out of the question, the kissing and hugging had to be out of the question too. Especially because she'd already determined that their first kiss hadn't been a fluke—that second kiss had been even better, so that she'd only wanted more of him, not less.

In fact, she could see how kissing him could become addictive. The more they kissed, the more they would want. And the more they wanted, the more they'd kiss. And where would it eventually lead?

She'd always wondered how women with self-respect could end up pregnant before marriage. But she supposed if such women had felt even half of what she'd just felt with Tanner, they could've easily tossed aside all reason.

But not her. She wasn't tossing aside a single ounce of reason. She wouldn't let herself kiss Tanner again. Twice was all.

"I'm an idiot." Tanner's voice was low and filled with self-loathing.

Was he having second thoughts about their kissing now too? Maybe he hadn't liked it. Maybe she hadn't kissed him as well as the other women he'd known—because surely a man like Tanner had kissed plenty of other women. He probably had women throwing themselves upon him everywhere he went.

The very image of him bending in and kissing someone else the way he'd just kissed her sent protest through her—protest she knew she shouldn't feel because Tanner didn't belong to her. He could kiss anyone he wanted. They'd both be better off if he did.

Tanner's fingers pinched the back of his neck. "I'm sorry, Maisy."

"Don't be." She tried to keep her voice light, but it came out breathless, and only then did she realize how winded she was from the kissing.

He turned to face her, dropping his hands and grabbing the stable railing. His brown eyes were darker than midnight. As he took in the heaving of her chest, he swallowed hard before casting his gaze down to the patch of yellowed grass in front of him, gripping the rail behind him even tighter.

A heated shiver raced up her spine. There was definitely something happening between them, something that had been unleashed—something that was powerful.

"I intended to comfort you." His words came out harshly. "And I shouldn't have kissed you."

She had to defuse this new tension. Otherwise he was gonna run away and never come back. And she couldn't let that happen. They'd been friends for too long, and she didn't want to lose him.

Before he could say anything more, she forced a laugh. "Tanner, hush up."

He glanced up and then immediately focused on the grass again.

"You're not at fault." She made her voice nonchalant—even though there was nothing nonchalant about this situation—because she sensed that one wrong word or move would push him away forever. "I'm the one who kissed you."

"You're grieving and vulnerable and not thinking straight."

Maybe he was correct. If she'd been in her right mind and not reeling from Nelly's death, maybe she wouldn't have fallen so easily into his arms. Maybe they wouldn't have been so close. And maybe she wouldn't have initiated a kiss.

Or maybe she would have eventually anyway. Because if she was completely honest, she'd harbored an attraction to Tanner Oakley since she'd met him. What woman wouldn't be attracted to such a charming and good-looking man?

Now that she was old enough to start thinking about men, he rose far above anyone else she'd known. He was everything she'd ever wanted in a man . . . except for one thing.

She released a tense breath. That one thing—his wandering ways—was an enormous obstacle, one she'd never be able to overlook or accept. And even if at some point Tanner decided to put aside his fur trapping and trail guiding to get married, he was too restless and too unsettled to stay in one place for very long.

Not that he wanted her. Just because he'd kissed her didn't mean he was thinking about marrying her. She was getting too far ahead of herself.

"Listen, Maisy." He straightened his shoulders as if bracing himself for what he needed to say. "I was wrong to kiss you. It was taking advantage of the situation, and I shouldn't have done it."

She waved a hand at him, trying to brush off his concerns. "I was curious about kissing you, that's all. And now that we've kissed, it's done and in the past."

She had to make it *done and in the past* for the reasons she'd just told herself.

He peered beyond her to the woodland bordering the clearing, as if he was hoping her pa and Glenn would come walking out. Yes, clearly he wanted to run away from all that had happened between them.

She couldn't let him leave like this, though—not without him realizing he didn't have to be afraid of anything. Because she had no intention—not even the smallest iota—of pursuing him.

He glanced inside the stable at his horse munching on hay.

He was just like all the other men in her life. He came and went as he pleased. Nothing ever tied him down.

"We'd better head on out." His voice was still tight.

"We?"

"Now that Nelly's gone, you said for yourself that you

don't need to live here."

So he wasn't planning on running away without her? She almost sagged with relief.

"I'll ride with you to Breckenridge," he continued, "and help you make arrangements to go to live with your aunt in Minnesota."

At his words, the relief evaporated, and dismay filled its place. Maybe he wasn't running from her, but he was trying to send her away real fast, which was just about the same thing.

Even if he wasn't pushing her away, she still couldn't leave today and *make arrangements* to go to Minnesota. She didn't have any money beyond a few pennies. She was gonna have to ask her pa for the cash to pay all the traveling fees. And if he said no, she'd either have to wire a telegram to her aunt and ask for help, or she'd have to find work in Breckenridge and save up.

But she wouldn't admit that to Tanner. She didn't want his charity or his pity.

The truth was, she could manage living in the mountains just fine on her own until Pa returned. Even without Nelly there. During those times when Nelly had been sick after miscarriages or the previous stillbirth, Maisy had shouldered everything. She knew how to do all the work and how to survive against the worst of the elements that came with mountain living—freezing temperatures, low provisions, dangerous wild animals, and more.

"I'm not ready to move." She was a strong woman. And she didn't need a man. "Reckon you'll need to go on without me."

Tanner shook his head curtly. "I can't leave you here alone, and you know it."

"I can't leave yet, and *you know it*. First, I need to tell Pa and Glenn what happened and where I'm going."

"Write them a note."

"Neither of them read. And even if they did, I can't go off to Minnesota without saying goodbye." She hoped her excuse sounded believable.

Tanner opened his mouth as if he wanted to object. But he knew as well as she did that even though her pa was gone for long stretches, he was a decent man and had always loved his wife and daughters. And in spite of everything, Maisy still loved him in return.

"He'll be crushed to learn of Nelly's death," she added, "and he'll be worried if he finds me gone."

"But if you stay too long, you might miss the chance to get out of the high country and to Minnesota before passes are covered."

"Then I'll only stay another week or two. They'll be home before too long." At least, she hoped so. And she hoped her pa would understand that she couldn't stay with him any longer. Maybe now, after losing Nelly, he'd realize she'd be better off living a normal life. Maybe he'd finally be willing to give that to her. She could only pray it would be so.

Lord in heaven above, help him.

He'd kissed Maisy Merritt, and now he couldn't think of anything else. Especially with the way she was standing there beside Nelly's grave with her hands on her hips, looking so feisty and beautiful.

Though her hair was plaited in a single braid, wisps of red hair curled around her face—her thoroughly flushed face. From the kissing.

Her lips . . . they were swollen. From the kissing.

Her chest . . . it was still heaving. From the kissing.

Her eyes . . . they sparkled with life. From the kissing.

Everything about her reminded him of their kissing and probably always would from here to eternity. Because the simple fact was, he'd never kissed another woman the way he'd just kissed Maisy. Or maybe it was the way she'd kissed him.

He should have known Maisy would kiss the same

way she lived—without reservation, holding nothing back, and with passion and enthusiasm.

Just thinking about how she'd nibbled at his lip sent another jolt of heat through his blood—a jolt he didn't need. Not if he had any hope of holding on to his sanity.

Her cheek was smudged with dirt and her eyes rimmed with shadows from her exhaustion. But everything about her face—every line, every freckle, every curve—was exquisite and stirred something deep inside him.

He wasn't sure what that something was—maybe attraction or need. Whatever it was, he was scared of it. And he wanted to put some distance between them so he could regain a measure of self-control. Because as long as he was near her, his self-control seemed to be slipping from his grasp no matter how hard he was trying to hang on to it.

"You may as well head on out." Her long lashes framed her wide eyes, making her impossibly irresistible. "I'll be just fine."

He tore his gaze from her. He didn't like the idea of leaving her alone. In fact, even when she'd had Nelly, he'd hated her being out here in the middle of the wilderness, a two-day hike from civilization. But he'd lived with his frustration for this long. What were a few more days or a week until her pa and Glenn returned?

"No, Maisy." As much as he wanted to get on his

horse and ride away, he'd never be able to do it. Maisy wasn't his responsibility, but he couldn't just allow her to fend for herself, knowing she was vulnerable and that anything could happen to her. He only had to think about her sitting on that ledge and unable to climb up to know that he'd never have any peace of mind if he left her.

The fact was, if she needed to stay a little longer, he'd have to stay too. There really wasn't any reason he couldn't. He'd only set about half of his traps. And he could ride out to check them easily enough from here.

Even so, he scrambled to find a solution that didn't involve staying at the cabin with her and putting himself into a tempting situation. But he didn't know what that solution was.

"Smoke will take care of me." She glanced at the wolf affectionately where he lay sprawled out at the base of the dead fir tree. At the mention of his name, the wolf rose to his feet, stretched his back, and then sauntered over to her. The presence of the wolf did give Tanner some peace of mind. But it wasn't enough.

She reached down and scratched him between the ears. "And I can handle Lester Acker just fine."

"What trouble is Lester up to now?" Tanner's tone took on a hard note as he peered off into the distance at the wisp of smoke rising from Acker's cabin.

Before Tanner left for New York City, Lester had

been pestering him about his trapping, accusing him of having too many traps along the river and forcing Lester and his sons to go out farther to hunt. The fellow had also given Cleveland a hard time about his traps, and he'd made it clear he didn't like Maisy's wolf—accused the wolf of making hunting more difficult and terrorizing his herd of cattle.

"Last week Lester rode up here and told me if he sees Smoke down along the river again, he's gonna hunt him down and put a bullet in his head."

"Then keep Smoke up here by the cabin."

"And how am I supposed to do that? Tie him up like a dog?"

"Maybe."

She sighed dramatically. "He'll never let me do that. He'll chew right through a rope. And I wouldn't do it anyway. He's still a wild creature and deserves to be free to come and go as he pleases."

"I'm sorry, Maisy. You know I like Smoke, and I'm indebted to him for coming after me yesterday. But he's a wolf. And wolves are bad for cattle. Plain and simple." Growing up as a rancher and now as a trapper, Tanner was accustomed to slaughtering animals for a living. And he wouldn't think twice about killing a wolf—for the pelt as well as the bounty.

She fisted her hand on her hip. "If Lester comes up here after Smoke, we're gonna have a war. *Plain and simple.*"

Tanner shook his head. "No, no fighting Lester—"

"Oh, I'll be fighting him. You bet I'll be pulling out all my guns."

"Absolutely not." Tanner's brows furrowed into a dark line.

She laid a hand protectively on Smoke's head. "I'm not gonna sit by while Lester kills Smoke. And you can't expect me to."

"I can and I will."

She stuck out her chin. "Try and stop me."

He jutted out his chin too. "Smoke's not worth it."

"He's worth it to me." She rubbed his snout. "Aren't you, boy?"

All the more reason he had to stay with her until her pa and Glenn got back. He couldn't leave her alone if trouble was brewing with Lester Acker.

"All right, I'll stay."

She lifted her blue-green eyes and fixed them on him with the full force of their magnetism. "You'll stay here with me till my pa gets back?"

"We'll stay for one week. And if he's not back by then, you have to promise you'll go with me."

She hesitated.

"Maisy." He leveled a stern look at her.

"Okay." She didn't sound confident. But he'd gotten her word, and that's all he needed.

The bigger issue at hand was the two of them being

alone for a week. "I don't like that we'll be unchaperoned. People will hear of it and talk."

"No one's gonna find out if we don't tell them."

He didn't want to compromise her reputation, that was true. But he also didn't want any more attraction to spark between them. He needed to go back to the way things had always been—friendly and flirty but with solid boundaries.

Maybe if he constantly reminded himself that she was five years younger. If he thought of her as a sister.

She was still petting Smoke and working her fingers around the wolf's neck in a massage.

Tanner couldn't keep from watching those fingers—the same ones that had clasped his neck, dragged him down toward her, and then pinned him in place with a force that had sent desire raging through him. He'd loved her taking control and doing what she wanted. In fact, just the thought of her bossiness sent that same heated desire shooting into his blood again.

She paused. "You're worrying for nothin'."

"It's not *nothin'.*" Frustration nagged at him. How could she be so cavalier about their kissing? "We kissed, and I don't want it to happen again."

"I don't either." Her gaze dropped to his lips and lingered there.

His body ignited into flames.

Blast. This was exactly what he didn't want to

happen. He didn't want to have these kinds of silent exchanges where he became extra aware of her and then his desires flared to life.

"I promise I won't kiss you again," she said adamantly. "I told you it's done and in the past, and I mean it."

He rounded the railing and brushed a hand over the soft flank of his gelding. His muscles were tight and his body on edge. The arrangement wasn't going to work. How could it? Not unless he could keep his distance from her. Only then would he have a chance at burying all his desires far underground where they belonged.

She released Smoke and started toward the stable. "If you think I'm gonna fall for you and beg you to marry me, you're wrong."

He wasn't worried about her so much as himself. But he couldn't say that.

"I told you I want a normal life, and that's something you'll never be able to offer a woman."

Never? Something inside him gave a beat of protest. He wanted to deny her, but he had no livelihood other than trapping and trail guiding. He had no home except a cabin in the woods. And he had no plans for his future.

The truth was, he'd never wanted to settle down, never had the desire to carve out a life someplace, never had aspirations for a career.

Maisy was right. He couldn't offer her or any other

woman a normal life. He was better off remaining alone.

She halted a few feet from the railing and stuffed her hands into her coat pockets. "Stop flattering yourself, big guy." The teasing was back in her voice. "I know it's probably a blow to your self-esteem, but I don't want to run off with you and marry you."

When she laid it out like that, maybe he was making more out of the situation than it warranted. They'd accidentally kissed. They'd stirred up some attraction to each other. But that's as far as it needed to go.

"Okay," he said. "We both agree that we don't want to be with each other and that the best thing to do is keep a friendship and nothing more."

"Yep." She nodded. "Friendship and nothin' more."

Friendship was all he needed with her. It had worked for them so far, and he would make it work in the future. "All right."

"All right." She smiled. "Thank you for being here for me, Tanner."

"Friends help friends," he added.

She studied his face for a moment, then gave him a tight smile. "I'm going to catch some shut-eye, *friend*." Without waiting for his response, she turned and walked to the cabin with Smoke on her heels.

When she disappeared around the corner, he expelled a long breath. Even though he was determined to view Maisy as only a friend, he suspected it would be one of the hardest things he would ever do.

Tanner is just a friend. Tanner is just a friend. Tanner is just a friend.

Maisy forced the words through her head over and over and kept her gaze from straying to where he was sitting at the table, repairing the hammer of his double-barreled shotgun.

She had to focus on frying the black morel mushrooms she'd uncovered and the grouse she'd shot that afternoon after she'd awoken from several hours of sleep. Tanner hadn't been around, and his horse had been gone. A part of her had suspected that he'd left her in spite of their conversation earlier. Because that's what men always did. They left.

But she was used to it. So in spite of the surge of disappointment, she'd taken her rifle and headed out to scavenge for food. After the past week of spending every spare moment at Nelly's bedside, she'd had little time to hunt. And with Pa and Glenn having been gone for so long, she was out of most staple provisions.

She wasn't worried about going hungry. Her pa had taught her enough over the years that she could survive. She could easily locate edible roots and berries. She could pull fish from any river or lake. And she knew how to find game, even in the winter.

When she'd returned to the cabin, she'd had a couple of grouse slung over her shoulder and a bag full of orache leaves, tansy mustard, and dandelion plants. She'd also found enough serviceberries for several meals.

Tanner had also returned and started working on gutting some marmots—he'd apparently headed out to check on some of his closest traps and brought back his catches. To say she'd been relieved to see him would be an understatement.

Now that darkness had fallen, he'd washed up and come inside. He'd fixed the broken latch on the door before setting to work cleaning and repairing his guns—a daily task for an experienced hunter like him.

All the while, their conversation had been normal and comfortable as always, and there hadn't been any awkwardness between them. He seemed to be doing exactly as they'd agreed—keeping to friendship and nothing more.

As he'd worked at the table, he'd told her about traveling to New York City with Ryder and his new wife along with Boone, Ryder's son. The trip accounted for where Tanner had been over recent weeks. He'd gone to meet with his investigator, who was helping him in his efforts to find his family. But apparently the meetings hadn't been as productive as Tanner had hoped.

She flipped a piece of the meat, the sizzling lard turning it crispy and brown. And she let herself sneak a look at him, bent over on the bench, the parts of his rifle spread out on the table before him.

Without his hat, his brown hair was wavy, curling at the nape of his neck. His shirt stretched tightly across his broad shoulders and around his biceps, outlining his muscles as he unscrewed a bolt.

His fingers worked at each part with certainty and dexterity—long fingers with blunt nails. Those fingers had skimmed up and down her spine. So softly, so sweetly. And she'd loved it.

Nope. She tore her gaze from him and forced her attention onto the pan. But all she could see was the darkness of his eyes after he'd kissed her. The blackness had enveloped her with delicious heat—so delicious that she'd wanted to bask in it forever.

Would she ever feel it again? She wanted to. But she couldn't with Tanner.

Because he was just a friend. *Tanner is just a friend.*

Once more she repeated the mantra, needing to convince herself of the truth. Why was it so hard to do so?

Was it because of the kisses they'd shared? She didn't want to relive them, knew doing so would make it harder for her to think of him as only a friend. But she couldn't keep her mind from wandering back to those few moments when her mouth had been pressed against his.

She'd never expected kissing to be so enjoyable. She'd never expected that attraction could develop so swiftly either. Now the wanting was burning low and steady inside her and refused to be extinguished no matter how hard she tried.

"And so that's it." Tanner finished his tale of Ryder and his new wife Genevieve. "They're sickeningly in love and can't keep their hands off each other."

Maisy didn't want to keep her hands off Tanner either, so she could understand Genevieve's difficulty. "That's not sickening. It's adorable."

Tanner guffawed. "It's not adorable when they're kissing every time you turn around."

"It *is* adorable."

Tanner didn't banter back. Instead, he grew silent.

She glanced at him over her shoulder to find that he'd stopped working on his gun and was staring unseeingly ahead, familiar shadows haunting his face.

"What are you thinking about?" She'd never held back from asking questions and pushing for answers. Nelly had often accused her of being too bold and sometimes even being a pest. But Maisy figured there was nothing wrong with asking questions—that it was up to the person on the receiving end to decide if they wanted to answer or not.

Tanner kept staring at the wall, and he seemed to be lost in thought.

She slid the skillet off the front burner to the back. Then she scooped up a large spoonful of the meat and mushrooms and deposited the mixture on a bed of greens she'd already arranged on his plate next to the glazed fruit she'd cooked earlier. She did the same for hers, then she crossed to the table and put the plates down.

The sight and scent of the meal drew him back to the present. He bent and dragged in a whiff of the food. "You're an amazing cook, Maisy. You can take anything and make it into a delicious meal."

She smiled at his words of praise. "Thank you."

"It's the truth." He picked up his fork and dug in.

She stood by the table, let him take one bite, then she asked her question again. "So, what's bothering you? That you didn't find your family the way you'd hoped?"

He finished swallowing, then dangled his fork above his plate. "I've decided to stop searching for my family."

Considering how important it was to him, he couldn't be serious—except that his expression *was* serious.

"You can't stop." She knew how much he'd wanted to find out about his past—where he and Ryder had come from and if they had any living relatives. "It's important to you."

"Not anymore." Tanner spoke the words with a resignation that Maisy didn't like.

"Course it still is. Now that your investigator knows your and Ryder's real names and those of your parents, it's just gonna be a matter of time before something turns up."

He took another bite of his meal, chewed, and swallowed before speaking again. "During my last few days in New York City, I realized something."

She pulled out the bench adjacent to his and sat down.

"I realized that Ryder and I have both handled the losses in our past in different ways." Once again Tanner stared at the wall, clearly trying to make sense of the pain of all that had happened to him as a little boy. "He kept trying to forget about it, while all I've done is try to remember it."

She'd only met Ryder twice, and while he was a fine-looking man like Tanner, he'd been reserved and gruff and temperamental. "It's okay to handle it differently. You're different than Ryder."

Tanner nodded. "Ryder's stopped trying to forget and is making peace with his past. Because of that, he's finally able to move on with his life."

From everything Tanner had told her, Ryder had

indeed moved on and was relishing his new life with Genevieve.

"If I can stop having to know everything and learn more, then maybe I'll be able to find peace too."

She reached over and placed a hand on his arm. The second she did so, he flinched and drew back, almost as though she'd scorched him. Then he shoveled in a mouthful of food.

She swiped up her fork and took a bite of her meal. How had it become so natural to touch Tanner? Should she apologize? On the other hand, why should she? She hadn't meant anything by it.

"You can't be so jumpy every time we touch, Tanner."

He paused in chewing.

"There's nothin' wrong with me patting your arm." Was there?

He swallowed, then blew out a breath. "I'm trying hard to forget all about what happened outside earlier today." He didn't have to say *the kissing* for her to know that's what he was referring to. "But since just looking at you makes it hard enough to forget, you touching me will make it impossible."

The same heat as earlier sparked again in the air between them. It was alive and magnetic and made her want to draw closer to him. How could her desire charge to life so easily after it had been stomped out earlier? Or maybe it hadn't died out. Maybe it was impossible to stomp out. Maybe it would always linger somewhere inside of her.

After all, Tanner was a pretty special man, and she doubted she'd ever meet anyone else like him. Granted, she hadn't met all that many men in her isolated life, but she didn't hold out too much hope that she'd find another man like Tanner once she reached Minnesota and her aunt.

"Can we agree to no touching?" he asked, his voice sounding strained. "No matter how innocent it might seem?"

Because apparently it wasn't so innocent . . . for either one of them.

Even so, she had to tease him and find a way to ease the tension between them. "So I can't do this?" She reached over and mussed his hair.

He sat up straighter, his eyes widening.

"Or this?" She socked his arm with her knuckles.

This time a slow grin worked its way up his lips.

"What about this?" She shoved at his chest.

"No. None of it."

Smiling, she picked up her fork again. "You're no fun."

He ate another bite through his grin.

She did the same. Even though she could never be in a serious relationship with Tanner Oakley, she'd always care about him. It was impossible not to.

8

Tanner tossed his bedroll to the floor near the stove and tried not to look at the bed, where Maisy was tucked away under the blankets.

He didn't want to ruin things now—not after how well the whole evening had gone. They'd had the one incident at supper when she'd touched his arm, but Maisy had somehow, as she usually did, managed to smooth things over and change the mood.

Her meal had been delicious—even better than some of the fancy meals he'd recently eaten in New York City that had been prepared by expert chefs. After supper, he'd finished cleaning his guns while she'd washed dishes. Then they'd played cards the rest of the night, her enthusiasm and competitive spirit making the time pass quickly.

He was struck again by how adept she was at living in the mountains, how strong and courageous and independent. She didn't really need him staying with her. She would have gotten on just fine by herself. But he felt better being there and making sure she was okay.

At least, he'd felt better until she'd asked him to step outside so that she could get ready for bed. All the while he'd fed and watered his horse, he'd thought of nothing else but the fact that she was inside the cabin shedding her clothes. He'd scrubbed his eyes to take away the picture, but he hadn't been able to stop his mind from wandering back to her.

Ever since he'd come inside, heat had been simmering in his gut. It hadn't helped that she'd been walking around in a nightgown, with bare feet and her hair flowing around her in stunning red waves. And she'd been as oblivious as usual to her beauty and sensuality and appeal.

He was glad he was the one there and not any other man. Because at least he had integrity and wouldn't try to take advantage of her.

A prick of guilt stabbed him as he kicked at his bedroll to flatten it. So much for his integrity. He had taken advantage of her when he'd kissed her earlier in the day. Even though she'd insisted that she'd been the one to start the kiss, he could have made sure it'd never happened or at least put an end to it right away.

Instead, he'd given in and kissed her as though he was a dying man and she was everything he needed to live.

Not only had he given in to the kiss once, but he'd kissed her again with even more passion.

As he turned to ready the stove for the coming night, he steeled his shoulders. He may have failed her then, but he wouldn't fail her again.

Smoke's golden eyes were following Tanner. The wolf didn't seem jealous or angry that Tanner was there. Instead, he almost seemed grateful—if that was possible.

"Read to me, Tanner." Maisy's voice was soft—too soft. It seemed to beckon to him so that he couldn't stop himself from stealing a glance her way.

She was sitting propped up with pillows against the log wall, the covers pulled up to her neck, and she was watching his every move just like Smoke.

Of course she was.

He swallowed hard.

Her eyes were so wide and innocent. Her hair was still loose. And her expression was much too welcoming.

What would it be like to slide in beside her and draw her into his arms?

His heart picked up pace, suddenly thudding hard against his chest.

What was wrong with him? He'd been with a beautiful woman for less than twenty-four hours and was acting like a love-crazed fool.

He grabbed a medium-sized log from the wood box, opened the stove door, and added the fuel. Had he been too rash to think he'd never take a wife? He couldn't deny that he had manly desires. And he couldn't deny that they'd been pulsing with full force since he'd pulled Maisy up from the ledge.

Maybe he needed to consider the possibility of having a wife after all. Of course, not Maisy. She deserved someone much better than him—someone who could offer her everything she wanted and more.

He shook his head. No, he couldn't take a wife.

"Why?" Maisy's voice held a pouting note.

"Because I won't subject a wife to this kind of life." He'd already explained his position on the matter, hadn't he?

She released a soft laugh.

He glanced at her again.

Her eyes danced with merriment. "You won't read to me because you don't want to subject a wife to this kind of life?"

His mind scrambled back over the course of the conversation, and he realized his mistake. She'd asked him to read. But his thoughts apparently had only one destination—her.

"We're not married, Tanner." Her voice was filled with teasing. "So I guess you're safe to read to me."

He closed the stove, then palmed the back of his neck, the heat working its way up to his scalp. "That's not what I was talking about."

"Oh?"

"I was just thinking about—" How good she looked in bed? How he wanted to hold her? How his desires were getting away from him?

She lifted her brows, clearly waiting for him to finish.

"Sometimes I think I might need a wife, that's all."

"Really?" Her question rose with a note of surprise.

Blast. He was making a mess of this whole exchange and embarrassing himself in the process. "But in the end, I know I can't have one."

"Why not?"

"I already told you. I agree with you, that this life isn't fair to a woman."

"Then don't do this anymore." She flicked her hand over the room, to the clutter and the ruggedness and the sparseness and all it signified.

"I don't have anything else."

"Sure you do."

He huffed out a frustrated breath. "Not everything is as simple as you'd like to make it, Maisy."

"It doesn't have to be as complicated as *you* make it. *Tanner.*"

He loved how smart and outspoken she was. But tonight she didn't know what she was talking about. "I've been wandering these mountains since I moved here. I don't know what else I'd do."

"You know ranching and horses—"

"I tried to be content on the ranch. I tried to be interested in the horses and the cattle and all the other responsibilities. But I never enjoyed it the way Ryder did. I always got restless if I stayed too long."

"You can take up another trade."

During the train ride back from New York City, he'd considered every possibility, had gone over every trade and job one by one. And he hadn't been able to see himself settling down and doing any of them—at least, not for long.

"I think I have to accept the fact that I'll never be content in just one place."

"You're skilled at so many things."

"Like what?"

"You can fix just about anything that's broken."

He shrugged.

"And you can track just about anyone or anything."

"Which is good for a mountain man but doesn't do much good elsewhere."

"What about being a lawman or detective?"

"Not interested in either." He'd thought about both. He'd even contemplated becoming a soldier. But in the end, none of it appealed to him. Maybe nothing ever would.

"Hmmm . . ." She was still staring at him with her keen gaze, as though trying to see deep inside his soul. "What do you enjoy doing the most?"

His thoughts went immediately to the few journals at his cabin as well as the box of journals in a closet back at High Country Ranch—which had been shortened by most folks to High C Ranch. Ever since he'd learned to read and write, he'd recorded his daily thoughts and activities onto paper. He'd wanted—almost needed—to keep a record of his life, maybe because he'd already lost a part of it and never wanted to lose his memories again. Now, after so many years, he loved his writing time every evening. It was one thing he looked forward to every day.

"I can see that you're thinking of something," Maisy persisted.

His family knew that he journaled. They'd given him blank notebooks over the years as gifts. He'd never been embarrassed about his writing with them, and he didn't need to be with Maisy now either. She was like family. So why was it hard to talk about?

She pushed up to her knees. "Tell me." Perched in the center of the bed with her nightgown pooled around her, she was ethereal, the glow of the lantern on the table highlighting her face and all its lovely curves.

Why did she have to be so pretty all the time?

He wanted to cross to the table to extinguish the light so that he could also snuff out his wandering thoughts, but instead, he made his way to the lone shelf on the wall.

"C'mon. Spit it out."

"You're so bossy." He picked up the worn copy of

Swiss Family Robinson that had belonged to Cleveland's late wife.

"Yep." Maisy's tone held the hint of a smile. "At least I have no trouble admitting what I enjoy doing most."

"What's that?"

"Bossing you around."

He couldn't hold back a smile. "You're good at it."

"Course I am. It's one of my best skills."

He swiped at the layer of dust on the cover. The book probably hadn't been touched since the last time he'd read it. When had that been? Probably earlier in the summer when he'd come up to check on Nelly and Maisy—one of the times when he'd spent the night and had read to the two before retiring to the stable.

He'd considered staying out in the stable this time, but the nights were growing too cold to allow that, and there was nothing wrong with him bedding down on the floor. He'd done it plenty of times in the past . . . except that in the past, Nelly had always been there.

He'd never been in the cabin alone with Maisy.

"So, will you tell me or not?" Her question held a hopeful note.

He pulled out a bench at the table and sat down. He flipped open the book, hesitating. But what did he have to lose by sharing something more personal with her? Nothing that he could think of. "I enjoy writing in my journal."

She was silent for a heartbeat, as if processing his revelation.

"It's not a big deal," he continued quickly. "I mostly write down where I travel and what I do."

"I can see you doing that."

"I know it sounds weird—"

"Not at all. I love that you do it."

"You do?" His gaze shot to her.

Her eyes brimmed with interest. "You've always been an amazing storyteller, regaling us with all your adventures. I'm sure they're just as interesting to read."

"I don't know about that."

"Read one to me."

"I don't have my journal with me." He'd come up to the cabin without anything except what filled his saddlebags, which hadn't been much—his bedroll, a clean shirt, extra ammunition, and a variety of metal parts and tools he might need for fixing traps. "Even if I had it, I wouldn't read it to you."

"Why not?"

"It's private."

"Like a diary?"

"No, but I don't let random people read my journal."

"I'm not random."

She was right—she was far from random. In fact, at times like this, he felt closer to her than he did anyone else, even Ryder.

He just shook his head and flipped through *Swiss Family Robinson* to the dog-eared page where he'd finished reading last time. He scanned the page, looking for a good place to start up the story again, perhaps rereading a couple paragraphs.

As he bent his head, something thwacked against his back. Even though it was soft, the force took him by surprise, and he toppled forward, the book slipping from his grip. Before he could turn around, the same item thudded into him again.

Was it a pillow?

He pivoted on the bench, and this time, the soft mound slapped him in the face. On the other side, Maisy stood a short distance from him. She swung the pillow away from him and held it motionless above her head while her blue-green eyes flashed at him.

"I won't stand for it." She jutted her chin adorably.

"Stand for what?"

"You telling me I'm random."

He crossed his arms and leaned back against the table, watching her through narrowed slits but still unable to keep from taking her in from her messy hair down to her bare toes.

Strange anticipation coursed through him.

She gripped the pillow as if she intended to swing it at him again. "Take it back."

"Or what?"

"Or this." She brought the pillow down on his head.

Before it connected, he blocked it and wrenched it from her grip. He bunched the pillow in his hand and stood. He'd always loved this playfulness between them. He loved that she was so unpredictable and endearing and unafraid of him.

Her eyes rounded upon the pillow in his hand.

He lifted it. Of course, he would never hit her hard. But he couldn't resist joining in the pillow fight. As he brought the mound down lightly toward her, she squealed and then ducked out of his reach.

At his miss, she laughed and scampered away from him toward the bed. "I just figured out something you're not skilled at," she taunted as she swiped up a second pillow.

"And what's that?" He advanced upon her.

"Pillow fights." She spun and clobbered him with the second pillow, then laughing again, she darted past him and out of his reach. She didn't stop until she was on the opposite side of the table.

He started after her, his blood racing faster. "Maybe I'm going easy on you. Did you think of that?"

She held her pillow up, her face alight with a beautiful smile—one he never wanted to forget. "Maybe I'm going easy on you too."

"I doubt it." He crept closer. When he was within reach, he swung his pillow at her.

She spun away from him and in the next instant pummeled her pillow against his back.

He grabbed for her pillow, intending to pull it from her and disarm her, but she slipped from his reach and raced away. He chased after her, going around the table several times before trapping her in a corner—or at least, he'd thought he'd trapped her, until she jabbed him with her pillow and got away again.

She was nimble and sharp, and by the time he finally got a handful of her pillow, they were both breathless and laughing. As he started to tug her closer, she released her pillow altogether, throwing him off balance so that he tumbled backward and fell on the bed.

Somehow she managed to gain possession of both pillows, whacking him and flattening him. He wrestled for control, but again, she proved herself strong and quick, and before he knew what was happening, she'd pinned both his arms to the bed.

"Take it back." She knelt over him and peered down at him with her bright smile and laughing eyes.

"Take what back?" He didn't care that he'd lost as long as he could see her happy face.

"That I'm random." She shoved his arms, then she sat down on him.

The moment her backside landed against his thighs, every coherent thought fled, and all he could think about was that Maisy was on top of him, straddling him, on the bed.

Heat speared him swiftly, and he stopped struggling.

Her red hair hung in a curtain around them, so thick and long and vibrant. And her nightgown had fallen off one shoulder, revealing miles of bare skin along her collar bone.

His throat dried up, and his smile and laughter fell away. His mind was stuck on one thought—Maisy was right there, her luscious body fitting against his. It would be so easy to lift a hand, tangle it in her hair, and pull her face down so that he could kiss her.

But he suspected that if he started kissing her now, he might not want to stop—not with how much his own body was suddenly aching for her.

As if sensing his drifting thoughts, or perhaps seeing his fading humor, her own smile disappeared. Her gaze dropped right to his mouth, and her eyes darkened. Her fingers on his arms dug into his flesh, and she sucked in a quick breath, drawing his attention to her chest, where the bodice of her nightgown was pulled tight and low, revealing a hint of her womanly figure.

Lord in heaven above. This was going from bad to worse, and he needed to put an end to their indecent situation before he lost every rational thought.

With all the strength he could muster, he rolled away from her, scrambled off the bed, and crossed to the table.

He braced both hands on the edge, partially to hold himself up and partially so that he could prevent himself from turning around. He was afraid if he took one look at her—even just a glimpse—he wouldn't be able to stop from walking back to her, throwing himself down beside her, and drawing her into his arms.

She was silent and motionless, as if she, too, sensed that the fire had ignited into scorching flames between them. It had gone from banked embers to forest-fire force in mere seconds. Even now, the air crackled with the sparks.

He closed his eyes, trying to block out the image of her from seconds ago when she'd been kneeling over him, smiling down at him, her beauty beyond words. But the image was seared into his memory. It was coursing through his veins. And he had the feeling it always would be—that no other woman would ever be able to compare to her.

He'd made a mistake in staying. That was clear. Because obviously, he couldn't keep from lusting after her.

Rapidly, before he could allow himself another look at her, he turned off the lantern, plunging the cabin into darkness. Then he sidled around the table and felt for the place he'd dropped his bedroll. It was shoved aside from all their running during the pillow fight. He made quick work of straightening it and then lying down and covering himself.

Only when he was on the hard, cold floor did he

finally allow himself a full breath. And only after she was sleeping a short while later did he unclench his hands from his bedroll.

He didn't understand what was happening to him and Maisy, but one thing was certain: her pa needed to return real soon before he did something he'd regret.

9

Maisy would never tire of the view of Tanner hiking in front of her.

She tromped in the fallen leaves along the river path behind him, a day's worth of game over her shoulder, and a day's worth of trappings over his. Glistening in the late-afternoon sunshine, the river flowed a dozen paces away, its rushing sound playing a melody with the rustling of the branches and the remaining leaves in the trees.

Tanner strode with a certainty and purpose she couldn't keep from admiring. And of course, she couldn't keep from also admiring his muscular back and shoulders. His fringed leather coat was taut across his arms, especially where he held his rifle. As he scanned the woodland with his keen gaze, she got glimpses of his profile—his angular jaw and cheeks, his perfect nose, and his scruffy, unshaven face. At certain times, when he held his chin higher or his shoulders straight, she could picture him as a wealthy gentleman. There was just something in his bearing that had always made her think he didn't quite belong here.

They'd traipsed around the wilderness for the past three days, and those three days had turned out to be the best of her life.

She was used to gathering food and hunting alone, so when Tanner had suggested they work together, she'd been hesitant. But she'd quickly realized just how much she loved spending the long hours with him. They'd hiked many miles each day, resetting his traps and then searching for food.

They'd always ended their days in time to return to the cabin and dress their game. Then she'd fixed them supper while he'd cleaned their guns. Afterward, they'd played cards, and once she was in bed and he was on his pallet, he read to her until she started yawning.

She'd tried to keep everything as friend-like as possible with Tanner since his reaction to the pillow fight. That night, he'd been so aloof that she'd been afraid he'd storm out of the cabin and ride away right then and there. As it was, he hadn't spoken with her until the next day after breakfast.

She knew he just wanted to be careful to keep their relationship from veering into a new territory that neither of them wanted. And she couldn't be upset with him for it. In fact, she had to be careful to keep the relationship from veering off too.

The pillow fight had shown her that she had to abstain from any physical contact whatsoever. Of course, Tanner had already tried to tell her that. But she'd felt the power of their attraction to each other again that night, and she'd done better since then.

But that didn't mean she couldn't enjoy looking at him—especially from behind, when he wasn't aware that she was staring. She'd just finished telling him about the young pygmy owl with the broken wing that she'd cared for a few weeks ago, and she'd been watching him the whole time then too.

He ducked under a branch and held it back for her.

She'd wound her hair under her Stetson and tucked her skirt up so that it wouldn't tangle in the brush. Under her heavy coat, her trousers showed along with her tall leather boots. She supposed that from a distance, someone could mistake her for a man. Usually she didn't mind looking so masculine, and it was probably for the best around Tanner.

Even so, a part of her wished she could put on a fancy gown just once and see Tanner's reaction. She wasn't sure why, except that he'd never really seen her at her best—had always seen her in tattered clothing with the dirt and dust of the mountain coating her.

"How are you holding up?" he asked, cutting a glance her way.

"I'm fine." Even if she wasn't, she wouldn't have told him. She had too much pride to admit to being tired or hungry—and she was both. "How are you holding up?"

He turned his head, but not before she caught the hint of a grin on his lips.

She hurried to stay up with him. "Do I amuse you?"

"Sometimes."

"What exactly about me do you find so amusing?"

"You're cute." He tromped forward without looking back. "That's all."

"I'm not cute."

"Sure you are."

She huffed, giving him a shove from behind.

He laughed, but the sound was cut short as he stepped into a clearing along the river and came to an abrupt halt. She moved beside him and scowled at the sight that met them.

Lester Acker and two of his grown sons blocked the path ahead—the one that led uphill to her cabin. Their feet were braced wide, and their rifles pointed forward.

Lester was the shortest of the three, with flat features—especially his nose, which had probably been broken one too many times. He never smiled, but he always showed his teeth, a few of which were discolored and others of which were missing entirely.

His oldest son, Lenny, who was around eighteen, could have been good-looking with his dark hair and eyes.

But there was something about him that Maisy didn't like—probably the way he always looked at her as if she were prey he'd like to trap.

The other son, Louie, was younger but also the largest of the three, with a bulky, giantlike body but a much kinder face than Lester and Lenny. He hardly ever spoke, and when he did, it was usually in one- or two-word answers.

She was tempted to point her rifle right back at her three neighbors, but she didn't want to lower herself to their level of intimidation. "Put your guns away, Lester. That's not the way to greet your closest neighbor."

"It is today." He ground out the words.

Tanner's grip on his rifle was taut, and his other hand rested on his revolver handle. "What's the problem?"

"The problem is that blamed wolf of hers." Lester scanned the woodland, as if searching for Smoke, probably expecting the wolf to come bounding along the trail after her.

But Smoke hadn't gone with her and Tanner. He'd actually been gone the past two days, probably doing his own hunting. Or perhaps with Tanner there to protect her, Smoke had sensed that he had more freedom to roam. Whatever the case, she was glad he wasn't around at the moment, because no doubt Lester and his sons would've shot him.

"The wolf mauled a calf today." Lenny threw out the

accusation as if it was the worst crime that had ever been committed in the history of the earth.

Tanner didn't say anything, but she knew what he was thinking—that her neighbors had every right to be upset if one of their calves had been attacked.

Even so, they had no right to blame Smoke. "You don't know if Smoke did it."

Lester continued to peer past her. "He's the only wolf I've seen around my place."

She rolled her eyes. "There's plenty of other wolves, and everyone knows it."

"And that's the problem." Lester shifted his rifle toward a moving shadow in the forest, but it was only a squirrel racing along a branch. "It's past time I took out that wolf and all the others around here before they destroy my herd completely."

"You're not killing Smoke." The words came out hotly with all the affection she felt for the wolf.

"Young lady, I'm done playing games." Lester leveled a serious gaze on her. "You shoot that wolf and bring me the carcass as proof—"

"You can't be serious."

"I'm dead serious." His expression remained grave.

"There's no way in heaven or on earth I'll ever kill him."

"Bring me his carcass by high noon tomorrow, or you'll leave me with no choice but to stake out your place and bring him down myself."

"You wouldn't dare." She started toward him as if that could stop him, but Tanner grabbed her arm and held her back.

"Don't try me." Lester finally lowered his gun, and his sons followed suit.

Tanner didn't release her, but she didn't try to break free either. What could she possibly do anyway? Hit Lester in the face? Shove him? Break his nose?

The truth was, she couldn't do anything.

Lester and his sons hiked toward the river, where their horses were tied up near the crossing—the place where the water was the lowest. "Remember," Lester called as he reached his horse. "Noon tomorrow. No later."

"You'll be waiting forever," she shouted after him. "I'm not killing my wolf."

"Then I'll be coming to do it myself," Lester called back. A moment later, he and his sons were mounted and heading away.

Only then did she jerk her arm from Tanner and start up the trail. She raced ahead of him, not wanting to hear his rebuke about Smoke. The fact was, Smoke very well could've mauled the calf. He was a wild predator who killed for his survival. It was only natural that he'd seek out a calf.

But she didn't want to shoot her wolf. Not when she'd raised him from a pup, and not when he was one of her closest companions in the lonely wilderness. Smoke cared about her just as much—maybe even more than she cared about him. She only had to think about the way he'd sought out help for her when she'd been stuck on the ledge. Or the way that he'd defended her from a coyote a few weeks ago. Or how he'd alerted her to a couple of strangers passing by and growled at them when they'd come too near her.

No, she'd never in a million years purposefully harm Smoke. Not after all they'd shared together.

If only she could communicate with him that he needed to go deeper into the wilderness and hunt farther away from civilization. Or even somehow tell him that it was time for him to break away from her altogether and start his own life, find a mate, and build his own pack.

Tanner followed her up the trail silently, which was fine with her because she didn't want to hear his rebuke at the moment—especially his voice of reason reminding her that Lester had every right to be upset. Any rancher would've wanted to put an end to the wolf problem.

They worked silently as they did their evening chores. All the while, she prayed Smoke would stay away, that he wouldn't return for another day or two. Then, when Lester came up to hunt the wolf down, she could tell her neighbor honestly that Smoke was away and she hadn't seen him recently.

But of course, the wolf came loping out of the woods

just as she finished gutting the small pheasant she'd shot. He bounded up to her, his tail wagging, eager for attention and affirmation. She could feel Tanner watching her as she rubbed Smoke's head. But again, he didn't bring up the confrontation with Lester—not until after supper was cleaned up and she was dealing a hand of All Fours.

"So, are we going to talk about Lester's threat?" He was leaning forward casually, his elbows resting on the table, his brown hair damp from dumping the remainder of the wash basin over his head before dinner. Now, without his coonskin cap, the locks lay in thick waves that beckoned her to comb them back with her fingers.

"There's nothin' to talk about." She finished giving them each their cards, then flipped up her first card to reveal a jack of diamonds.

He didn't pick up his cards, and she could feel his intense gaze upon her.

She pushed his stack closer. "C'mon."

"What do you plan to do?" Tanner's tone was calm but contained a firmness that warned her he wouldn't be swayed from talking about the issue any longer.

With an exaggerated sigh, she slapped her cards down on the table. "I'm not doing anything. Lester will calm down by tomorrow and this won't amount to anything." It certainly wasn't Lester's first threat, and it probably wouldn't be his last, unless she left with Tanner at the end of the week. And she still hadn't made up her mind to go, even though she'd told Tanner she would.

"And if Lester doesn't calm down?"

"I'll tell him the same thing I told him today. He's not killing Smoke."

Tanner glanced at Smoke, now sprawled out on the floor in front of the door in his usual spot. "I know you have a bond with him, but he's not worth the fight, is he?"

"Yep." She pushed up from the bench and fisted her hands on her hips. "Yep, he's worth it."

Tanner's eyes were filled with questions that demanded answers—like what she planned to do with Smoke when she moved out of the mountains.

"I don't know what I'll do with him." She couldn't keep the frustration from her voice. "But you can't expect me to kill him, can you?"

Compassion creased Tanner's forehead and the corners of his eyes.

There were times when she turned around in the cabin and expected Nelly to be standing there, waiting to listen, eager to hear about all her adventures. But her sister's sweet smiling face was gone forever, and now everyone wanted her to sacrifice Smoke.

Tears stung her eyes. "He's all I have left, Tanner. Once he's gone, I have no one."

"You still have me." His reply was soft and sincere.

Yet, as nice as it was, they both knew the truth. After she left Colorado, even after she left the mountains, she wouldn't see him often, if at all.

"I have to defend him," she said, unable to keep her voice from wavering.

Tanner hesitated, then nodded. "Okay. If that's what you want to do, I'll help you."

She lowered herself back to the bench, swallowed the sorrow that threatened to overwhelm her, and prayed Lester wouldn't follow through on his threat.

# 10

Noon had come and gone, and Tanner hadn't seen a sign of Lester Acker and his sons. At least, not yet.

The early afternoon sun had climbed high in the sky, chased away the chill in the air, and turned the day balmy for October. The bright light was shining on the eastern hills beyond the river and turning the changing leaves into gold, so that the beauty of the landscape was stunning.

And peaceful. Too peaceful to fight against an angry neighbor.

But Maisy had made up her mind to defend Smoke. And once Maisy made up her mind, he knew there was no swaying her. She was strong-willed and determined, and she'd fight to keep Smoke with or without his help.

As much as he understood Lester Acker's frustration over losing his cattle to wolves, he also understood that Maisy counted Smoke as a friend, almost as family. And she wouldn't stand by and let anyone hurt the creature.

Like it or not, he would have to help her save Smoke.

And now they were both staying near the cabin . . . just in case Lester followed through on his threat.

Tanner deposited the wood he'd brought in, adding it to what was stacked near the wood box. Maisy stirred one of the pots filled with the stew she'd set to cooking shortly after dawn with the remaining pheasant she'd shot yesterday.

He prayed they wouldn't have to fight Lester, but he feared the fellow wouldn't be satisfied until Smoke was gone.

Was there any other solution to the problem?

Tanner stood back, crossed his arms, and stared at the wolf sitting in the corner where Maisy had positioned him a short while ago. How long would the creature stay before growing restless?

Smoke flattened his ears and peered back with his bright gold eyes. He seemed to be asking Tanner the same question: how long would *he* stay with Maisy before becoming restless?

Maisy cast him a glance over her shoulder, giving him a view of her beautiful face, now taut with worry. "Thank you for helping me, Tanner. I'm indebted to you."

"Yes, you are, darlin'." He forced a smile, hoping to lighten the gravity of the situation. "And I intend to make you pay for all this help."

An easy smile formed on her lips. "And what kind of payment are you expecting?"

"A big one."

"Meat enough to last you a week?"

"No. Something better."

"Meat and greens?"

"No, even better than that." He wanted to steal a kiss. But he couldn't admit to that.

He hadn't teased her much over the past few days, and he missed their bantering. But he'd been attempting to refrain from thinking about his desire for her and hadn't wanted to do anything that would allow his feelings to surface. That meant he'd tried to keep from staring at her, watching her, thinking about her, and flirting with her.

He'd had to set strict guidelines for his own sanity.

But now, at this moment, he could sense she needed to be distracted from the worry of protecting Smoke. He could set aside the stringent rules he'd given himself the night of the pillow fight, couldn't he? Just for a little while?

She turned to face him, sipping the liquid on the spoon at the same time.

She had such a pretty mouth—her bottom lip rounded and plump and her top lip defined and full with a perfect dip in the middle.

It wouldn't hurt anything to admire her again,

especially since he'd done well so far keeping his rules. Surely he could make this exception and let himself enjoy looking at her mouth.

She sipped at the hot liquid, blew on it, then sipped again. "I think I can guess what you want."

"I doubt it."

"I have no doubt." She lifted the spoon back to her lips and this time licked at the remaining liquid.

At the sight of her tongue, heat pierced him low and hard. He knew he needed to focus on something else, but he couldn't tear his gaze away.

As she licked again, this time at the drips off the side of the spoon, her lips curved up into a taunting smile.

His breathing had snagged inside, and he tried now to draw in air. But her tongue flicked out over her upper lip, and he couldn't make his lungs work, not even a wheeze.

When she lowered the spoon, she laughed lightly. "I'll give you the payment you want. Have no fear."

He finally tore his gaze from her mouth to find that her eyes were dancing merrily. He'd nearly forgotten what they were talking about—clearly a common problem around her. Since he wasn't sure he could get his voice working without it cracking, he cocked one of his brows.

"Don't think I can't tell." She smiled so broadly that he couldn't imagine a more beautiful sight in all the world. "A blind man in a blizzard could tell."

"What?" he managed.

"That you want to kiss me again."

Was it that obvious? He almost choked and made himself look away, this time out the wide-open door. He immediately tensed. Several horses and riders had crested the rise, and several more seemed to be joining them along the clearing at the trailhead.

Lester had brought a posse, which meant he was aiming to get Smoke one way or another.

With a surge of resolve to stand by Maisy through the confrontation, Tanner grabbed his rifle from the table where he'd left it and unholstered his revolver from his belt. As he stepped into the doorway, he made sure both of his guns were visible.

"Tanner Oakley." Lester's greeting was less than friendly. Not that the man was ever all that friendly—not with their disputes over the trapping grounds.

"Lester." Tanner spoke the man's name without any preamble or welcome. At the same time, he counted six men, including Lester's oldest sons—Lenny and Louie. Tanner recognized two of the others as miners from down in One-legged Joe's Mine. The third was a stranger, but Tanner guessed he was the newest rancher who'd moved into the river valley.

Shouldering his rifle, Lester stepped forward with a scowl. "Was hoping I was wrong about my suspicions about you staying up here with Cleveland's daughter."

Tanner's gut pinched with the guilt he'd been

attempting to hold at bay. "It's not what it looks like."

Lester's oldest son, Lenny, guffawed.

Lester shot him a dark look that silenced him and left him sullen. Then he turned his forbidding glare upon Tanner. "Reckon Cleveland ain't gonna be happy when he learns you've been staying here fornicating with his daughter."

Tanner stiffened at the insult against Maisy. "I'm here as a family friend. That's all."

"He's made it clear through these parts that he'll cut up and dismember any man who touches his girls."

Tanner was well aware of Cleveland's threats. But that was to scare away all the other men, not him. Cleveland trusted him and knew he wouldn't take advantage of Maisy.

Regardless, he'd wanted to avoid the speculation and rumors. But what could he do now except to justify why he was there and hope the explanation was enough? "His older daughter died this week. I didn't want to leave Maisy alone."

"You'd have been better off if you had."

"If you must know, I'm sleeping on the floor. Maisy's just a friend. That's all."

"All I got to say is that Cleveland's gonna kill you." Lester didn't crack a smile. Clearly this was no joking matter to him.

Even so, the fellow had it all wrong, and Tanner

wanted to prove it. Yet how could he? All he had was his word.

"Now, let's get down to business." Lester surveyed the cabin yard and the stable beyond. "I came to see if you have the wolf carcass I asked for."

The other men had dismounted and now formed a line behind Lester, all of them armed.

Tanner didn't want to stir up more trouble, but he didn't owe these men anything. And he owed Smoke a chance at living since he'd been the one to save Maisy's life this week.

Thankfully, Maisy was still inside, crouched beside Smoke, both arms around him. Clearly she intended to guard the wolf and make the men shoot through her first.

Tanner sighed. "Listen, Lester. Maisy is moving out of the area real soon."

"Then all the more reason to kill the wolf."

"No." Tanner spoke the word firmly, decisively. "She's taking the wolf with her. And it won't be a problem after that."

Lester was silent for several beats. One of the men— the new rancher—leaned in and spoke in a low but urgent tone. Lester nodded several times before facing forward again. "You know as well as I do that wolf will make his way back here eventually. No sense putting off the inevitable."

"He's a loyal creature. It's possible he'll stay with her."

"You should know I can't chance that."

The problem was, Tanner did know it. He'd killed his share of pesky wolves over the years to keep the Oakley cattle and horses safe. But this time was different. Because of Maisy.

"Sorry, Lester, but we're not handing the wolf over. You might as well go on home." With that, he closed the door and latched it.

"Come on, now," Lester shouted. "I don't want to hurt either of you."

"Then go home," Tanner called through the door.

"I'm not going without that carcass."

"Guess we're at a standoff."

Silence settled outside. Tanner didn't think Lester would purposefully hurt either him or Maisy, but the situation was still precarious.

Was the wolf worth the danger?

No. He shook his head and turned to tell Maisy so.

She was still kneeling next to Smoke, both of her arms around the creature and her eyes wide with fear.

He didn't want to let her down. And giving Smoke over to Lester would hurt her more than anything. He couldn't hurt her in that way. He cared about her too much.

"Go home, Lester," he called again. "We promise to keep the wolf in the cabin until we leave the area."

"I've given the girl and the wolf enough chances, and

I'm done." Lester's tone rang with finality. "We'll be waiting out here until you open up and surrender . . . however long that takes."

Tanner had hoped it wouldn't come to this. But he and Maisy could wait things out for a short while. Lester and his crew would get cold and tired and leave soon enough.

Maisy curled up on the floor next to Smoke, stroking the wolf's haunches.

Long hours had passed since Lester had shown up at the cabin with his sons and friends. In some ways, she supposed she hadn't really expected him to carry through and come after Smoke, since he'd been all threats and no action in the past. But not only was he carrying through, he also wasn't leaving.

She didn't want to think about what would happen if the fellows stayed indefinitely. Maybe she and Tanner should have left the area this morning instead of waiting until the end of the week. Then she could have taken Smoke away before getting trapped in this impossible situation.

But the truth was, she hadn't taken the danger as seriously as she should have. She guessed Tanner hadn't expected this kind of a showdown either.

Across the unlit cabin, Tanner shifted his position next to the front window that overlooked the cleared rise. Now that darkness had fallen, they couldn't see Lester or anyone else.

The men had taken up positions surrounding the cabin so that no matter which of the two windows Tanner looked out, someone was always watching in the distance with a gun pointed at them.

They were stuck. That's what.

But Tanner had reassured her that Lester and his men wouldn't last long before they gave up. They'd soon grow weary of going without beds and food and the other comforts of home. And the dropping temperature of the night wouldn't be pleasant either.

Meanwhile, she and Tanner were cozy and warm inside the cabin, even though they had to wander about in the darkness because Tanner didn't want to light a lantern and give the fellows outside an easy shot at them. Not that the men would actually shoot at them. Lester wouldn't let the situation get that out of hand.

"Why don't you go to sleep." Tanner's whisper cut across the cabin.

He hadn't seemed happy with her since the moment the men had shown up earlier in the day. She couldn't blame him. If she'd left the mountains earlier in the week the way he'd wanted, they could've avoided all the problems, not only with Smoke but also with the rumors about them.

Lester's accusations had been mortifying to hear, and it had taken all the self-restraint she'd been able to muster to keep from storming outside and telling him how it really was. The only thing that had held her back was the fear that Smoke would follow her.

Course, Tanner had tried to defend her, had explained everything well enough. The trouble was, Lester already had his mind made up that she and Tanner were guilty of *fornicating*.

Now the rumors would only grow and spread, and she'd have a tarnished reputation for sure. No one would believe she and Tanner were innocent, that nothing had happened between them.

Her pa would trust her though. At least, she hoped he'd be rational about the whole situation and realize Tanner had stayed with her out of the goodness of his heart and not because he'd wanted to take advantage of her.

"Go on now," Tanner insisted. "You may as well get a little sleep."

She sat up on the floor beside Smoke. "You sleep first, and I'll keep watch."

"No. I'm trying to figure out how many men Lester's planning to keep awake." The moonlight revealed Tanner's outline as he peered through the slit in the curtains. His shoulders were rigid, his gun still in hand, and his jaw hard.

"I can keep a lookout too."

"I'm hoping that once the men head off to sleep, we'll be able to sneak out one of the windows and make it down the mountain."

A small whisper of hope broke through her despair. "Do you think we can?"

"We've got to try it. Once we're down by the river, we'll be able to make it to Breckenridge and then to High C Ranch. You'll be safe there."

She wasn't worried about herself, but she knew Tanner was more concerned about her safety than Smoke's.

Silence settled in the room again.

Smoke nudged her hand with his damp nose. She returned her fingers to his neck and dug in, scratching him where he liked it best. She guessed the wolf sensed the unrest and danger but didn't realize he was at fault. And it wasn't really his fault. If he really had killed Lester's calf, he was just being a wolf and hunting for his food.

"I'm sorry, Tanner." Her words were laced with all the regret that was growing inside her. "I shouldn't have involved you in any of this."

He was silent for another beat before answering. "I'm relieved I'm here and that you don't have to face Lester alone."

"I'm glad you're here too." He was the only one who

would fight off neighbors with her for the sake of her wolf. If her pa and Glenn had come home, they would've shot Smoke to keep the peace. Of course, they wouldn't have given Lester the pelt and would have kept it for the cash for themselves.

"I can't guarantee that Smoke will make it out alive," he said softly. "But we'll do the best we can to save him."

"You're the kindest and sweetest man I've ever known." Her words came out more impassioned than she'd intended, and once they were hanging in the air, she could feel her face flush.

"Not sure if that's a compliment." His whisper was laced with teasing. "How many men do you know? Three? Four?"

"I know plenty." She kept her voice sassy, hoping to hide her relief that he wasn't upset—or at least, was trying to make her feel better. "Even if you're overly hairy at times, I know a good man when I see one."

"Overly hairy?"

"Do you even know what a haircut and shave are?"

"I did both before going to New York City, so I have a vague recollection."

"You're in need of both again, so you're in luck. I'm willing to do them for you."

"No."

"I've been giving my pa his haircuts for years."

"No, Maisy."

"Not tonight, of course. But once we're through all this—"

"Never." His voice took on a rumble that did strange things to her insides. "I'm already having a hard enough time keeping my hands to myself. Let's not make things worse."

He was having a hard time keeping his hands to himself? "What does that mean?"

"You know."

She guessed he was referring to her, but she wanted to hear more, wanted him to clarify, wanted to know what he really thought of her. "If I cut your hair, I'd be the one touching you, not the other way around." She wasn't above pretending ignorance and baiting him to say more.

He was silent for several beats. "Your touch is like fire," he finally whispered. "If I get too close to you, I burn up."

She smiled, loving that she had that kind of power over him. But she didn't want him to sense her satisfaction. Instead, she continued her innocent act. "I'm sorry. I didn't realize it was so disagreeable to be near me."

He snorted. "It's too agreeable. And that's the problem."

She could feel her flush deepening. "I guess that means you'll be happy when you don't have to be around me anymore."

"Of course not. I've always loved spending time with you. It's just more challenging now that you're all grown up and so beautiful."

"You think I'm beautiful?"

"More beautiful than any other woman I've ever known."

Her stomach was doing multiple flips, which threw her off balance. She drew her arms around her knees, hugging herself close. Tanner thought she was more beautiful than any other woman he'd known. The revelation was incredible and amazing . . . and even intimidating.

"More beautiful than the three or four women you've known? Reckon that's not hard to do."

He scoffed. "I've known plenty of women, darlin'. And you top them all." Somehow, his voice ended on a tender and sincere note—one that made her wish things were different between them.

"Thank you, Tanner." Had they been less stubborn about what they both wanted, they might have had a chance to see where their relationship led. As it was, they were going opposite directions—he didn't like being tied down, and she wanted permanence and stability.

Her thoughts flew back over the past few days she'd spent with him in the wilderness. He'd included her in everything he'd done, brought her along, treated her as an equal, and hadn't left her behind. She'd loved every minute with him, whether they'd been resetting his traps or climbing mountain trails.

Her heartbeat clanged to a noisy halt. Love? Why was she thinking of love at a time like this? Was it because she was falling in love with Tanner?

That wasn't possible, was it? Not after being together for so short a time.

Her gaze strayed his way again, to his rugged outline in the moonlight. She loved everything about him from his unshaven face and scraggly hair to his corded body and blazing eyes. More than that, she loved who he was deep inside—his generosity, compassion, and helpfulness. She could spend countless hours with him and never tire of being with him or talking with him. He was interesting and witty and fun to be with.

Yep, she was falling in love with him. Maybe she'd been in love with him long before this visit. Maybe she'd always loved him but had just been too against his mountain-man ways to admit it.

Could she put aside her resistance to be with him? Could her love for him overcome all the other issues and differences they might have?

Maybe.

She sat up, sweet longing pulsing through her.

At her abruptness, Tanner's head swiveled in her direction. "What's wrong?"

What could she possibly say? She couldn't tell him

that she was having second thoughts about leaving Colorado, because she wasn't, was she? And yet, how could she possibly walk away from him? Not after this week and what she'd experienced with him. She couldn't imagine a future without him in it—didn't want to imagine it.

"What if I don't go to Minnesota?" She tossed the question out tentatively.

He paused, as though her reply was the last thing he'd expected. "Where would you go instead?"

"I'll stay in the area."

Even though she couldn't see his expression, she could sense the intensity of his posture and knew he was listening to her as carefully as always and taking what she had to say seriously—just one more thing she loved about him.

"Maybe I don't want to go too far away," she added.

"Don't do this, Maisy." His voice held a note of warning.

She pushed forward with what she wanted to say anyway. "Maybe I want to be with you, and maybe we shouldn't worry about all the reasons we aren't right for each other."

"They matter."

"They don't have to."

He released a tight breath. "We already decided to go our separate ways."

"We can change our plans."

"I told you that I refuse to subject a woman to the life I lead."

"What if she's willing to join you anyway?"

"You already told me you want a normal husband and a normal life. Those were your words, Maisy, not mine."

"I know." She could admit she still wanted normal. But at the moment, she wanted Tanner more. Was this what it had been like for Ma? Was that why she'd married Pa? Because she'd loved him enough to sacrifice her own desires to be with him?

There had never been any doubt that Ma had loved Pa and had been happy when she was with him. The trouble had been the rest of the time when he'd been gone. She'd been sad, just going through the motions of living, and hadn't come to life until Pa was home again.

Maisy resented that her ma's happiness had revolved around a man. She'd frequently wished over the years that Ma could've found some joy in being with Nelly and her. But they'd never brought Ma the same satisfaction and reason for living that Pa had.

Maisy had never understood why. But now that her feelings for Tanner were growing so rapidly, she could begin to empathize a little more with what her ma had felt. And maybe it was foolish to even consider walking down the same path as her ma.

"It probably wouldn't work," she finally said. "So

don't worry about it."

"I agree." His voice was still tight. "It's for the best not to consider it."

She expelled a sigh. As if sensing her inner battle, Smoke lifted his head and gave her a sloppy kiss. She pressed a kiss back to his face.

All the while, through the darkness, Tanner's stare was unyielding. Finally he shifted his attention out the window and blew out a tense breath.

She wasn't sure what to think of their exchange and Tanner shutting her down so completely. Part of her wanted to take Tanner's advice and not consider the option of being with him. But another part wasn't ready to let the issue go.

She supposed she first had to figure out what it was she really wanted. Did she want a life with Tanner? If so, then she wouldn't let anything deter her from it. Not even him.

12

Tanner inched the coat-disguised broom through the open window. With dawn only a couple of hours away, he and Maisy needed to make their escape soon.

For most of the night, he'd witnessed movement along the perimeter of the clearing in the moonlight—the glint of a gun barrel, the smolder of a cigar, the flickers of a campfire. He'd also heard the voices of men calling out to each other once in a while. But over the past hour or so, the night had grown quieter, and he hadn't seen anyone on the east side of the cabin.

He pushed the broom out farther, using it as a decoy. If anyone was watching the window, they'd likely think it was him trying to slip outside. And he wanted to see what they'd do.

Maisy had awakened after a couple of hours of sleep, and now she stood behind him, her heavy wool coat on and her body almost brushing his with how close she was.

He paused with the broom halfway out and strained to hear any voices or calls of alarm. But the silence of the night was heavy, the distant rushing of the river below the only sound.

"I think we can go," he whispered, moving the broom again.

In the next instant, a shot rang out. He jerked back just as a bullet split the glass in the upper windowpane. Pieces cracked, several toppling out of place, falling, and crashing against the floor.

He drew the broom inside at the same time that he flattened himself backward against Maisy to protect her. The move pushed her into the log wall so that his back was against her chest.

For long seconds, they didn't move. He'd already dropped the broom and had his revolver in hand.

"Do you think they'll shoot again?" she whispered.

"I don't think they're aiming for us." He sized up the spot where the bullet had shattered the glass. It was high enough in the window that whoever had taken the shot hadn't meant to hit him, had only wanted to prevent him from leaving. Or they had terrible aim, which wasn't likely since most men who lived in the wilderness had to become proficient hunters or go hungry.

"Lester and his men are sending us a message that they don't want to hurt us, but they're serious about holding us hostage until we give them Smoke."

Behind him, she remained motionless, her body tense. "Does this mean we won't be able to sneak out?"

"I don't know." From the careful surveillance the men were keeping, it didn't look as though that plan would work. But he wasn't giving up hope yet.

Lester's raised voice from outside called across the distance. "There's only one way out of the cabin, and that's with a dead wolf in hand."

Tanner could feel Maisy getting ready to shout something back. He spun and clamped a hand over her mouth. "Don't say anything."

In the moonlight streaming through the window, her eyes appeared wider than usual.

She mumbled something, was probably chewing him out.

He pressed in closer until his mouth was near her ear. "The less they know about what we're doing, the better."

She stilled and then nodded.

Slowly he lowered his hand from her mouth and at the same time holstered his revolver, but suddenly he was conscious of the feel of her loose hair against his jaw and how close his mouth was to her ear and her cheek. All he had to do was move a fraction and his lips would brush her skin.

Even though the situation was dangerous and uncertain, he was conscious of every breath she took, because her chest rose and fell against his. He hadn't pressed against her too forcefully, but he'd drawn closer than he should have.

He didn't move, couldn't force himself to back away even though he knew he needed to.

She didn't budge either.

Her words from earlier in the night came back to taunt him, as they had already a dozen times since their conversation. *Maybe I want to be with you, and maybe we shouldn't worry about all the reasons we aren't right for each other.*

She'd basically told him that she was willing to have a relationship with him. Maybe not in those exact words, but she'd made it clear that she was interested in him and whatever was developing between them—enough that she'd consider changing her plans.

He couldn't let her change her plans, could he?

She shifted a fraction, and her nose grazed his neck.

A wave of desire slammed into him, nearly knocking him breathless. He lifted his hands to either side of her body, boxing her in, and at the same time, he lowered his head so that his lips touched her ear.

She drew in a trembling breath and let her lips skim his neck.

The touch set him on fire. He leaned in closer to the hollow of her ear and kissed her hard.

She gave a soft murmur as she grasped his shirt. And then her lips pressed more fully to his neck.

What was he doing? He couldn't kiss her like this. It would only lead down a path he couldn't follow. He closed his eyes and fisted his hands to fight against all the longing coursing through him.

There was no denying how strong the need for her was growing with each passing day. He didn't understand the intensity of it, but he guessed the attraction was a result of being with her constantly. He'd rarely had a moment away from her since arriving. The more time he spent with her, the more qualities he saw in her that he liked, and there had already been plenty to begin with.

She was an incredible woman in so many ways . . . which was why he had to keep his distance from her. He couldn't give in to this momentary weakness. He had to stay strong for her sake. She deserved much better than he could offer.

Sure, she might be able to cast aside her dreams of having a normal husband and normal life because she was feeling the strong magnetism this week too. But if he let her do that, eventually she'd grow resentful of him, of her life, of what she'd given up.

He took a rapid step back from her. But she was clinging to his shirt and didn't let him get far. "Don't push me away again, Tanner," she whispered, standing up on her toes and kissing his neck once more.

"We can't be together, and you know it." He ought to cross to the other side of the room and put some distance between them, but her lips on his neck sent a charge all the way from his head down to his feet, immobilizing him.

"We can if that's what we want." She raised her face and this time skimmed his lips with hers.

He nearly groaned with all the need for her that he'd tried to hold back.

He was tired of resisting, tired of denying himself, tired of being strong when all he wanted was her. He wanted to kiss her and maybe never have to leave her again.

Was that even possible?

He let his mouth fuse with hers deeply as his hands slid up her back, eager for the feel of her beneath his fingertips. He craved her more than anything else, even more than his sanity—which he was obviously losing fast.

Her lips met his with a heated passion and desperate rhythm that matched his, as if she was trying to get as much of him as she could before he was torn away from her. In fact, her hands balled his shirt tighter, as if she had no plans to let go anytime soon and was demanding that he stay there.

He loved her bossiness even in her kissing and loved knowing that she was eager for him. It only seemed to ignite something deeper inside him—something that made him want to claim her and never let any other man even look at her. It was as if each beat of his heart thudded out "Mine, mine, mine."

But was she really his? He had no right to her now or anytime—not without being married to her. And he couldn't marry her, could he? Yes, she'd said they could do whatever they wanted. But once he was gone and she had the chance to think about the situation, she'd come to her senses and realize he wasn't the man for her.

At another call outside, he broke the kiss and took a rapid step away.

"I don't want anyone to get hurt," Lester was saying, "but next time you try to leave the cabin, we won't miss."

The threat hung in the air, as cold and clear as the breeze now blowing in through the broken window. It sent a chill up his backbone, and he dropped his head, the futility of their situation weighing heavily upon him—the futility of trying to save Smoke and also the futility of trying to have a life with her. Both were impossible. And he was a fool to think otherwise.

She slipped her fingers into his.

"No, Maisy." His whisper was harsh, and he pulled back, moving his hand out of her reach.

"Yes, Tanner." She attempted to grab his hand again.

She was a stubborn and determined woman, and when she set her mind to something, she rarely failed, even when nursing a wounded creature.

But he was quicker than she was, and he dodged away and rapidly crossed to the opposite wall.

"After that kiss, how can you keep pushing me away?" Her whisper was filled with hurt. "You can't tell me that you don't feel everything too."

He couldn't deny her. But the real problem was that he had nothing to offer her—not when he didn't know who he was or where he'd come from or what he wanted. He was a lost man with an empty past, an empty present, and an empty future.

The truth was, he'd always been lost—had never really belonged anywhere, not even at the Oakleys'. And maybe that was why he'd needed to find out more about his past. Maybe he'd believed that if he could discover where he'd come from, he'd have an easier time discovering where he needed to go.

But that hadn't happened. And in his heart of hearts, he was still as restless and unsettled as always, maybe even more so.

"We're good together," she said earnestly. In the dark, he could see her outline, and her petite body was rigid. "We make a good team."

"The problem isn't you. It's me."

"I don't understand. You're a wonderful man, Tanner. I can't imagine meeting anyone I like better."

He shook his head, trying to find a way to explain himself. But how could he when he could barely make sense of everything? "I don't know what I'm feeling."

"I think you're falling in love with me."

Was he? He'd never been in love before, but he imagined it felt very close to all that he was experiencing with her.

"And I think I'm falling in love with you," she added softly.

He rubbed the back of his neck. Their relationship was quickly heading into a new territory that they didn't need to go to. He had to rein them in and put a halt to things before she had him down on one knee proposing marriage.

And as stubborn as Maisy was, no doubt she'd have them engaged before the night was through.

He couldn't let that happen. Not yet. And maybe not ever.

Clenching his jaw against his mounting frustration, he glanced around the room. Smoke was standing and watching him, his ears drooping as though he knew the outcome of the night and was prepared for it.

The wolf knew it and so did Tanner. So why put it off? Besides, if he wanted a way to push Maisy away, this would do it.

He tugged his gun loose.

Having started to follow him, she froze by the table at the center of the room. "What are you doing?"

"I'm doing what I should have from the start."

"You're not killing Smoke."

"There's no other way."

13

Tanner was gonna shoot Smoke.

As she stared at the revolver he'd unholstered, time stood still for several heartbeats, and her mind flashed with her options. She was too far away from Smoke to jump in front of him and keep Tanner from hitting him.

But she was only two steps from the door. Lester's words from only moments ago echoed in her head: "*. . . next time you try to leave the cabin, we won't miss.*" She could cause a distraction, and maybe with the chaos of the moment, Smoke would have the chance to get away.

She took a rapid step toward the door. "Don't give up yet, Tanner."

He lifted his revolver and focused on the wolf.

"Please." Why was he doing this now? After helping her this long, what had changed? Maybe she'd pressured him too much, and now he was angry or frustrated. Or perhaps he wanted to escape from her and realized he'd create a chasm between them if he killed Smoke.

Whatever the case, she had to act quickly. She reached the door, unlocked it with one swift flip, and then threw it open so that it slammed hard against the cabin.

Tanner's attention immediately flew to her. "Maisy, don't you dare—"

She bolted out, the cold night air striking her cheeks.

The bang of a gun echoed in the quiet of predawn from somewhere near the trailhead. And in the next instant, a bullet hit her in the shoulder.

For just an instant, she seemed to hover in a place between space and time. She saw a man step forward into the clearing with his rifle smoking and another man beside him with his rifle aimed and ready for another shot.

Behind her, Tanner shouted a warning.

Then the pain drowned out every other thought. The sting was so intense she couldn't make her lungs work to draw in a breath. Heat followed—a searing that burned with so much force that a scream escaped before she realized it.

She stumbled forward, sinking to her knees, unable to bear the pain and still screaming.

At the scream, shouting erupted from the woods, and men came running out of their hiding places toward her. Tanner was the first to reach her, and he dropped beside her, his brow furrowed and his face tight with worry. He was scanning her, but in the dark, he was having a hard time finding the place where she'd been hit.

Through the chaos, Maisy glanced back into the cabin. Smoke stood in the center of the room, tense and alert, his golden eyes upon her.

She bit down to stop her screaming. At the same time, she held Smoke's gaze, and she silently pleaded with him to go. *Go, go, go. Run for your life.* He took a hesitant step forward, as though he was contemplating coming to help her.

She gave a curt shake of her head. And again, she urged him with her eyes to flee while the men were distracted. She'd done this for him. Yes, she'd expected gunfire, but she hadn't believed that anyone would actually shoot at her—not after Tanner's reassurance that the men weren't aiming for them and mainly wanted to scare them.

Even so, she needed Smoke to know she was making this sacrifice in order that he could live. He had to run away, stay safe, and make the sacrifice worthwhile.

Smoke gave a subtle nod, almost as if he understood what she was trying to communicate. Then he hesitated only a moment longer before turning and racing to the broken window that was wide open. In a graceful leap, he arched through the open lower half and disappeared outside.

With all the men hurrying toward her, she prayed none of them would spot the wolf bounding away—or at the very least that he would make it to the cover of the woodland before being noticed.

As Lester knelt on the other side of her across from Tanner, his focus was entirely upon her, and none of the other men called out alerts either.

She had to distract them for just a few more minutes, had to keep them from realizing Smoke was gone in order to give the wolf time to make it far enough away that the men wouldn't be able to track him and hunt him down.

It wasn't difficult to make more of a scene than she already had. She clutched at her shoulder where the bullet had entered. And once again, she was all too aware of the blazing of her flesh. It was so intense that she rolled to her side and vomited in the grass.

Tanner's hands clutched her arms as she heaved. "I can't believe you guys shot Maisy!" He was shouting at Lester.

"I told everyone to shoot but to miss!" Lester shouted back.

"Then why'd they hit her?"

The raging of the argument sounded far away as dizziness and pain threatened to blacken her mind and send her into oblivion.

"Where's she been hit?" This was a different voice, one Maisy didn't recognize.

"We need some light," Lester called.

"Maisy?" Tanner's face appeared above hers. "Where are you hurt?"

Unable to get the words out, she lifted a hand on her uninjured side and pointed toward her shoulder.

Tanner nodded and then began to gently peel back her coat. He halted abruptly, and at his murmured exclamation, she guessed he'd found the spot. She could feel the cold air on her shirt, which was damp and sticking to her body, likely from the blood she'd already lost.

Nausea swelled again into her throat. She twisted her head and vomited again, the movement and the pressure only adding to the unbearable burning.

"How bad is it?" Lester asked.

Tanner was bent over the spot, inspecting it. She could feel his hand on the underside of her shoulder too. "It didn't go all the way through, which means the bullet is lodged inside."

Lester cursed.

"She's bleeding a lot," someone else remarked.

Tanner rattled off a list of supplies for people to bring to him. And before she knew what was happening, she was being lifted and taken inside the cabin. Whoever was carrying her deposited her onto the bed. Someone else lit the lantern at the center of the table, and one of Lester's sons was scrambling about, putting water to boil.

Amidst the continued chaos, she finally heard someone mention that Smoke was nowhere to be seen. Lester cursed again, but then just shook his head. "This was all a bad idea anyway. I should've just put out the poison in the calf's carcass the way I'd planned."

She hated that some of the ranchers resorted to poison to kill the wolves. They used strychnine that looked like salt, and they often sprinkled it inside a dead buffalo or other dead prey that wolves hunted. It would attract a whole pack of wolves and kill them all pretty quickly.

The use of the poison had diminished the population of wolves along the Front Range to a minimum. But in the wilderness of the high country, the wolves deserved freedom from ranchers and other settlers encroaching on their hunting land.

She was just glad that, for now, Smoke was safe. Realistically she knew that he would always face danger in the wild—if not from the ranchers who wanted to eliminate the threat of wolves, then from other wild animals, disease, or hunger. But he was special to her and always would be.

Tanner hovered above her again, and he brushed her hair back from her face. "I'll bandage your wound as best I can to staunch the flow of blood, but I'll need to take you into town to the doctor so he can remove the bullet."

She nodded.

"It'll be a long ride." His voice was laced with regret.

Why the regret? Because he'd pulled out his gun to kill Smoke? And because she'd done what she had to in order to prevent him from injuring, possibly killing, her wolf?

His expression held an apology, but she closed her eyes to block him out. She didn't want him to apologize now—not after he'd rejected her. She'd declared her love for him, and he'd thrown it back in her face as if it meant nothing to him. Even if he hadn't liked it or had thought it was too soon, he could've talked about it maturely instead of turning against her. His reaction had been completely unexpected and had hurt her more than anything else he could've done.

The ache swelling in her chest didn't have anything to do with the bullet wound. It was the ache of a broken heart, a heart that was bleeding, a heart with the life draining from it.

And she was spitting mad. If she hadn't been flat on her back in bed, she would have jumped up and punched Tanner in the arm and then given him a piece of her mind. As it was, she could hardly move without scorching pain racing from one end of her body to the other.

"As soon as you bandage me up, I'll take your horse— if you'll let me—and I'll head out."

"I'm going with you."

"I can do it myself."

"You'll probably be too weak."

"Don't matter." She didn't care if she was being difficult or irrational. "I don't want to be with you."

He released a sigh. "Maisy."

"It's the truth."

"And I'm sorry." His voice dropped.

"Don't apologize. I don't want to hear it."

He was silent a beat. "Fair enough."

At the commotion of someone bringing Tanner the doctoring supplies, she turned her head away from him. A moment later when he bent back over her, she kept her face averted and answered his questions as briefly as possible.

As he cleaned the wound and bandaged it, she found herself fading in and out of consciousness, the pain too much to bear at times. When he finally had her shoulder and arm wrapped securely, he bundled her in several blankets before carrying her outside along with a bag of her few possessions.

Dawn had broken, and daylight hovered above the eastern peaks, thin wisps of clouds tinged with the pink of the rising sun. Frost coated the trees and brush, turning the wilderness into paradise.

Even though she was dizzy and weak, she swept her gaze over the landscape. This was goodbye. Once she rode away today, she didn't intend to return. She was done with the mountains, done with her life there, and done with waiting for Tanner to reciprocate her feelings.

She'd try to get in touch with her aunt in Minnesota and work something out. If she couldn't make the arrangements, she'd somehow get in touch with Pa once he was back, and she'd beg him for the fare to travel there.

After Pa made it home, she had no doubt that Lester would visit and relay his version of all that had happened. Pa wouldn't be happy about any of it, but maybe it would give him even more incentive to help her move away.

She wanted to climb up into the saddle without Tanner's help, but she was too shaky and weak to stand on her own, and she was forced to accept Tanner's assistance. When he situated himself into the saddle behind her, she was tempted to tell him to get off and walk, but with all the other men watching them, she reined in her anger.

As they started out, she could tell Tanner was trying to keep his gelding steady so that she wasn't tossed around too much. But no matter how carefully the horse stepped, each move jarred her.

When they finally reached the level path along the river, tears streaked her cheeks. She wasn't sure if the crying was from leaving home or Tanner's rejection or the pain. Maybe it was a combination of all of it.

When he brushed his thumb across one of her cheeks, she almost leaned into his touch. A part of her desperately needed him—his comfort, his assurances, and his strength. But another part of her despised him for letting her believe he might care about her, for letting her get close, for letting her hope in a future with him.

Granted, he'd never once made her any promises. All along, he'd been cautious—had warned her he didn't want to be more than friends and had tried to refrain from physical contact. He'd treated her respectfully, without crossing any lines.

If anyone was to blame for their situation, she was. She'd been the one to initiate their kisses, and she'd been the one to push for more.

Even so, he shouldn't have been so stubborn and shouldn't have treated her with such disregard, as if she meant no more to him than a passing fling.

As his thumb moved to wipe her other cheek, she turned her head away so that he couldn't touch her again. She was too tired and weak to do more than that. But it seemed to be enough to send him the message that he'd made his decision not to love her, and now whatever relationship had been developing between them was done.

She was done.

"How are you holding up?" he asked.

"I've been better."

"Let's see if you can handle it if I speed up." He nudged the horse to a faster trot. "I'd like to get to Breckenridge tonight, if possible."

As the jarring increased, she couldn't keep from

wincing. It would be a long and difficult ride, and already she was weary of the journey after just an hour.

"Is this pace okay?" His question rumbled near her ear.

"It's fine." She didn't care that her voice was clipped or that she was stiff or that she was uncommunicative.

They rode for several beats of silence before he heaved an exasperated sigh. "I'm sorry, Maisy—"

"I already said I don't want to hear your apology."

"I know. But I owe you one anyway."

She closed her eyes.

He clearly took her silence as permission to continue. "I never should have kissed you or led you on—"

"I get it, Tanner." She didn't want to hear his regrets—not when she'd loved kissing him and wished it could've all turned out differently. "You don't care about me and don't want to plan for a future together."

"I do care—"

"Not enough."

"I care enough to know that I'm no good for you, and even if you think you want to change your plans now, someday you'll regret it. And I can't let that happen."

She was too weak and weary to argue with him. Besides, maybe he was right. Maybe she'd been deluded by the stirring of her emotions over the past days together along with their closeness and the fact that it had just been the two of them.

If she had the chance to think about everything rationally and logically, she'd probably come to the same conclusion.

"You're right." She released a breath—one that contained all the sadness over the loss of their relationship. "I was mistaken to think I could have a future with you."

"Exactly." His response sounded forced and unconvincing.

Or maybe she just wished that was the way it sounded. Even so, she had to let go of the possibility of having Tanner in her life. As wretched as that thought made her feel, she should've known it wouldn't work out.

"As soon as you drop me off, I give you permission to ride out of my life."

"I don't want to do that—"

"It'd be for the best—especially for me, so that I can put you out of my mind."

"Okay." His response was hesitant. "If that's what you really want."

"Yep. It really is." It wasn't what she *really* wanted. But apparently what she really wanted was unrealistic and unattainable. And now she had to let him go. Not that he had ever been hers to begin with.

He lapsed into silence, and she did too. And thankfully, she drifted off to sleep, the exhaustion along with the pain and the loss of blood finally taking their toll.

14

Tanner wanted to shout out his frustration. Maisy had lapsed into unconsciousness, and he hadn't been able to rouse her for the past hour.

Ahead, he could see the faint lights coming from town—probably from the saloons and hotels that were still open and busy at the late hour. He was almost there after nearly fourteen hours of traversing the long mountain trails to return to civilization.

He'd had to go slow to keep from jostling her. The few times he'd stopped to give the horse a break, he'd checked her bandage, and at least her injury hadn't been bleeding too badly. She'd slept most of the day, rousing once in a while for him to give her sips of water. But clearly, her body had taken all it could handle.

Even though the ride had taken him longer than usual, it was almost over. He just prayed the doctor was home, because the wound site needed to be treated before it festered.

"We're almost there, darlin'," he whispered against her head, which was resting on his chest. She'd tried hard, whenever she'd been awake, to keep herself from sagging into him, but she'd grown weaker, and now he was holding her entirely within his embrace—to keep her comfortable and warm.

All throughout the long hours of the ride, regret had chased him, catching up with him plenty of times. He'd replayed that last minute together in the cabin, when he'd broken away from her, stalked across the room, and let fear take control. He'd been afraid of what was happening between them. He'd been afraid of the danger of their situation. And he'd been afraid of making mistakes that might cost him too much.

No matter the fears, he shouldn't have pulled his revolver out on Smoke. He should have talked to Maisy first.

He glanced over his shoulder. Smoke was keeping to the shadows but had been trailing them the whole ride out of the mountains. Tanner had caught glimpses of him from time to time.

Now as he peered over the foothills he'd left behind, the moonlight illuminated the swells of earth, mostly barren except for a few boulders and dry brush and sage. He couldn't see any movement or any hints of light.

Everything was silent. There wasn't a single wild creature in sight—probably because Smoke's presence had scared them away.

He shifted forward and nudged his gelding into a gallop. With the weight of two people, the horse was tired, but it kicked up its pace anyway.

Maisy released a soft moan, the increased pounding likely making her more uncomfortable again.

He pressed a kiss to the side of her head. He was taking a liberty in kissing her that way, and he never would have considered doing so if she'd been awake. She was angry with him over all that had happened, and she would have shoved him.

And he wouldn't have blamed her for pulling away or telling him to stop. He had no right to kiss her, even just her head. But that didn't keep him from wanting to kiss her or from thinking about the kisses they'd already shared.

The truth was, after that last kiss in the cabin, he'd known deep inside that everything in his life had changed as a result of being with her this time. Maybe a part of him had realized he'd eventually kiss her. After all, he'd always liked her, always flirted with her, always enjoyed her company. Even though he may have rationalized his feelings away after each previous visit, the attraction had been building all along.

With a sigh, he adjusted his hold on her so she rested

against him as comfortably as he could manage. A few minutes later, he reached the outskirts of town and slowed his mount. Most of the houses and businesses were dark with slumber. And maybe the doctor's would be dark too.

But Tanner pushed forward anyway toward the white clapboard building halfway down Main Street. A light burning from inside the front window cast a glow on the sign next to the door that read: *E.P. Howell, M.D. Physician and Surgeon.*

Hopefully the light inside meant Dr. Howell was still awake and wouldn't mind the interruption at the late hour.

Tanner reined in his horse, climbed down, then settled Maisy in his arms. He hurried up the front stoop to the door. Finding it unlocked, he opened it and stepped inside.

The front room of the doctor's office resembled a parlor, with a settee and wingback chairs and several end tables positioned to face a fireplace, which was dark and cold. A small bookcase sat against one wall, with old newspapers stacked on one shelf and medical journals cluttering the other. Another wall contained a collage of photos of people—presumably the doctor's family, although Tanner had never asked the older man.

Light came through the open door of an adjacent room—what might have been a dining room if it hadn't been transformed into an examining room.

"Dr. Howell?" Tanner called, too worried about Maisy to wait.

"Be right with you," the older man called from the examining room.

Tanner crossed to the door and peered inside.

Dr. Howell, a short man with gray hair that seemed to perpetually stick up, stood on a step stool beside a man who was getting stitches in his scalp. At the sound of Tanner in the doorway, Dr. Howell glanced up from the suture and thread he was slipping into a layer of bloodied skin.

"Tanner Oakley," the doctor said in greeting as he pulled the thread through. "Who you got there?"

"This is Maisy Merritt, Cleveland Merritt's daughter."

Dr. Howell made a humming noise as if he was trying to place the names. He snipped at the thread. "Doesn't sound familiar."

Tanner hadn't expected it to. Cleveland hadn't been around town much since moving to the area. He hadn't been around much at all. If he'd been home, the neighbors wouldn't have resorted to a shoot-out to get Smoke.

And maybe Maisy wouldn't have gotten hurt. . . . Even though Maisy hadn't talked about why she'd stepped outside the cabin, he'd figured it out easily enough. She'd hoped for some gunfire to distract the men while Smoke slipped out the window. And her plan had worked, except that she'd gotten hurt in the process.

Whatever the case, Tanner's anger toward Cleveland had boiled the entire ride to Breckenridge.

It didn't matter now, though. All that mattered was getting Maisy the help she needed.

"Maisy took a bullet to her shoulder."

While the doctor finished tying off the stitches, Tanner gave him the details of Maisy's gunshot and the hours that had passed. As soon as the other fellow was off the examining table, the doctor began calling out instructions for what to do with Maisy.

Although Tanner wasn't proficient in medical procedures, he'd seen enough accidents over the years to assist the doctor during Maisy's surgery. Even if he hadn't known a single thing, he still would have stayed and helped.

After administering ether to dull Maisy's pain, the doctor was able to extract the bullet with forceps. Because of how long the lead had remained inside her shoulder, the doctor was concerned about the wound festering, especially since it was already irritated and swollen. So instead of suturing the flesh closed, he packed it with a clean cloth.

When the surgery was finished, Dr. Howell instructed Tanner to carry Maisy to a bed in the room across the hallway where she would stay for the remainder of the night. When she was settled and resting, Tanner pulled up a chair beside the bed and insisted he was staying for the night. Not even Dr. Howell's raised brow could deter him.

After having been awake all the previous night, Tanner found himself dozing from time to time, his eyelids growing too heavy to keep open. Fortunately, Maisy didn't stir—not until dawn, when the ether began to wear off.

In the morning, Dr. Howell gave Maisy an opium painkiller before cleaning the wound again. Since there wasn't much more they could do for her besides wait for her to heal, Tanner decided that he would take her to High C Ranch to recuperate.

At least there he would be able to stay with her and tend to her without people gossiping about their relationship and making an issue of him staying by her bedside. Because that's what he intended to do. He wasn't leaving her side until she was better.

She slept most of the way there. This time he'd positioned her sideways on his lap, cradling her more fully against his body to keep her steady.

As they neared the ranch gate, she opened her eyes, lifted her head from his chest, and glanced around at the cloudy gray morning. "Where are we?" Her voice was groggy, and her pretty blue-green eyes were glassy.

"We're almost at High C Ranch."

Her lips curved into a half smile. "I've always wanted to visit your family's ranch and see all the horses."

"Well, darlin', I'm making your wish come true."

Her smile inched higher. "Will I get to see any foals?"

"Of course." The foals that had been born in the spring and early summer weren't babies any longer, but they were still young and beautiful and full of spirit. "But first, you have to get better."

"I'm feeling just fine." Her eyes remained glassy, and her face was flushed.

"The doctor gave you a lot of medicine, so hopefully that's helping." He was grateful she didn't have to suffer so much from the pain anymore.

"I don't remember seeing the doctor." She laid her head back against his chest as if holding it up was too much work.

So far she hadn't resisted sitting on his lap or the close proximity in general. He could only hope that meant she wasn't angry with him anymore.

"Dr. Howell removed the bullet last night, and now you just need some time for the wound to heal."

She didn't respond, and when he glanced down, her eyes were closed, her long lashes resting against her cheeks. She'd obviously fallen asleep again, which was for the best. The doctor had said she needed plenty of rest.

He situated her more securely in his arms, then bent and placed a kiss against her temple. He'd found himself all too easily kissing her head or hand over the past hours. And he knew he shouldn't give in to the need, but under the duress of the situation, he'd made excuses for doing so—especially because she was asleep and wouldn't realize he'd kissed her.

"Thank you, Tanner," she whispered.

He swiftly pulled back. Blast. He should have waited another minute to make sure she actually was asleep.

"I wouldn't have made it here if not for you," she continued softly.

He chanced another glance at her face to find that she was peering up at him, her eyes wide and filled with admiration. There was no sign of anger or irritation that he'd kissed her head. Although he knew he deserved her wrath, he didn't want to part ways as enemies. At the very least they could go back to the way things had always been between them, couldn't they?

"You saved my life." She lifted a hand to his chest and rested it above his heart.

"You probably wouldn't have been hurt in the first place if not for me."

"That's not true." She tilted her face, and she was suddenly at just the right angle that her lips grazed his jaw.

He stiffened at the contact. It was just an accident. That's all. Even so, the merest touch of her lips had the power to heat his blood.

Her lips brushed against his jaw again, and she released a breathy sigh. "Oh, Tanner, you feel so good."

Maybe the contact hadn't been an accident. Whatever the case, her touch, her groan, her words added more fuel to the heat that had started pumping through him. It was all too easy with Maisy to unleash the attraction.

But he couldn't. Hadn't he learned his lesson from staying at the cabin with her? He'd hurt her once, and he couldn't do it again.

Her fingers skimmed up his chest to his neck. "I think I could kiss you all day long," she whispered, her voice still groggy.

As bold as Maisy was, this confession was too much, even for her. The medicine was loosening her tongue.

"Don't you think you could kiss me all day too?" She made a trail to the back of his neck and then sifted through his hair.

The talk of kissing and the feel of her was more than he could bear. He clamped his mouth closed and fought against the need to drop his hand and skim up her arm and touch her hair too.

"Just kiss me, Tanner," she murmured against his jaw.

15

Tanner tried to put some distance between himself and Maisy, but it didn't work. Not with her sitting squarely on his lap.

Maisy definitely wasn't in her right mind. If she were, she wouldn't be trying to entice him—not after everything that had happened.

As much as he loved it when she bossed him around, and as much as he loved kissing her, he couldn't do it—wouldn't do it—when she wasn't thinking straight or fully cognizant.

Her lips dropped to his throat, and the pressure was hot and hard and demanding.

A hungry growl rose in his chest, but he rapidly swallowed it. Even as he did so, fresh desire swelled inside him. One little kiss wouldn't hurt, would it?

No. He shook his head. Absolutely not.

"Don't you want to kiss me?" Her voice held a note of indignance.

He didn't want to hurt her feelings by rejecting her outright. He'd already done that once, and he didn't want to do it again. Yet he had to refrain. He just needed to do so carefully. "Of course I want to kiss you, darlin'." He infused his tone with flirtation. "But I'm saving that kiss for a special occasion."

"A special occasion?" She released her grasp around his neck and curled against him so that her head was resting against his chest and her mouth out of reach and out of sight.

He exhaled a tense breath. "I'll make sure it's really special."

"I'd like that."

The truth was, there wouldn't be a special occasion for kissing her. Not anytime soon and not ever. All he planned to do was make sure she was healed from her gunshot wound and help her get settled someplace secure and safe. Then he would return to his life. In fact, maybe it was time to move on from his cabin on the lake. Now that she would no longer be living in the mountains nearby, what reason did he have for staying in his place?

A strange thought pushed to the front of his mind. He hadn't been staying in the area just for her, had he?

No, of course not. He hadn't moved on yet because his cabin had been within half a day's ride to visit Ryder.

But now that Ryder was no longer at his ranch and hadn't yet made plans to return, Tanner didn't have to take his brother into consideration.

In fact, at their parting in New York City, Tanner had finally released Ryder from the responsibility of caring for him. His big brother had shouldered the burden long enough, and Tanner had wanted to set him free to pursue his own life with his new wife and baby.

Not that he didn't want to see Ryder again. He did. And he hoped they could stay connected. But now that Ryder had a new life and purpose, Tanner didn't have anything tying him down anymore. And maybe that meant that he needed to move to a new location.

He'd heard the trapping was plentiful farther west in Colorado, where there were fewer settlers. But maybe it was too late in the autumn to consider moving. He might not have time to get settled somewhere and build a solid cabin to withstand the winter—especially if he stuck around to take care of Maisy.

He glanced down at her. She was so delicate and beautiful that just looking at her made his chest ache.

So what if he had stayed in the area because of her? There was nothing wrong with that, was there? He was being a good friend to look after her, especially now, in the absence of anyone else in her life.

He veered his horse toward the ranch gate—smooth log beams that were connected like a large door post and surrounded the wide metal gate. The top log above the gate contained the words *High Country Ranch* in black metal letters.

Split-rail fencing ran the length of either side of the gate, bordering the wide pastures that made up the Blue River Valley. High C Ranch had some of the best and most fertile fields in the area, making it ideal for grazing horses and cattle. Pa Oakley had recognized that over fourteen years ago when he'd brought his family west from Kentucky to Colorado to start a horse farm.

It had been on the Oakleys' journey to Colorado in a covered wagon that he and Ryder had first met the family. At the time, Tanner had been nine and Ryder eleven. They'd run away from their last orphanage in New York City because Ryder had been growing too old to stay in the system.

Before that last orphanage, whenever they'd faced the risk of being split apart, Ryder had found a way to make sure they stayed together. He'd always figured it out—even the times when they'd been taken into the country to live with farm families that needed extra help.

But when Ryder had been ordered to go to an industrial school, Tanner had been too young to go with him. The orphanage workers had insisted that they had no choice but to live separate lives, that it would work out just fine, and that they would still get to see each other once in a while. *Once in a while* hadn't been enough for Ryder.

Ryder had packed their bags that same night, and they'd sneaked out and never looked back. They'd spent weeks stowing away on steamers and trains until they'd reached Independence, Missouri. Finally, they'd hidden in a supply wagon heading west.

At the time, Tanner hadn't understood what Ryder was doing or where he was taking them. Maybe Ryder hadn't realized what he was doing either. But now, looking back, the journey made sense. Ryder had wanted to go west in a covered wagon because that's the last place they'd been with their parents. And maybe subconsciously, Ryder had hoped he'd find their parents or perhaps find the part of their lives that had been lost.

But Ryder hadn't been able to remember anything about their past or their family, and the trip hadn't brought any of the memories back, not even the smallest hint.

They'd been discovered in the supply wagon, and thankfully the Oakleys had taken them in and invited them to travel with them to the high country of Colorado and help start the new ranch.

Tanner didn't know what other options they'd had—probably none. So they'd joined the Oakley family and had never left. When the Oakleys had suggested adoption, Ryder had agreed immediately. Tanner hadn't been so sure that he wanted a new family, because he longed for his old one, but he'd gone along with it because that's what he'd always done—follow wherever Ryder led him.

Tanner could admit that living with the Oakleys had been one of the biggest blessings that ever could have come their way. Pa Oakley had been a kind but firm man and had helped shape both him and Ryder into hardworking, responsible men. Ma Oakley had been equally kind and also nurturing and had poured love into them just as easily as she had her own four children. All the siblings had been accepting, opening their hearts to two lonely kids who'd been in desperate need of stability and friendships and family.

Over recent months, since Pa and Ma had died, their family hadn't quite been the same. And Tanner missed them both, with their wisdom, peace, and love.

But even now, with Maisy injured and in need of a place to live, Tanner had no doubt Maverick and his wife Hazel would help him. And Clementine would too. They would welcome Maisy without any reservations, and they would let her stay as long as she needed because they were kind like that. And because they loved him and would do anything to make him happy.

Tanner urged his gelding down the long dirt road that wound about a quarter of a mile before reaching the main house and barns, which were situated along the foothills of Tenmile Range. He couldn't see the buildings from the road—not past the pine trees that provided a buffer against the wind and weather. But the steady curl of smoke rising from the house came into view and greeted him as it did every time he came home.

Within minutes, he was reining in near the house, which was a sprawling log structure that was, surprisingly, just as sturdy now as when it was first built. With large logs and solid chinking, the home, with its large windows, was picturesque against the mountain backdrop.

Maverick stepped out of one of the two main barns—the mare barn—across the ranch yard. With dark hair and blue eyes, he'd always been a favorite among the local women. In addition to being good-looking, he was a charmer and a big flirt, which was partly how Tanner had learned to flirt—because he'd watched Maverick do it so well.

Now, with his usual swagger and wide smile, Maverick headed across the ranch yard toward him. "Look what the cat dragged in."

"Howdy to you too." Tanner usually liked bantering with Maverick, but not today. He wasn't in the mood for anything but getting Maisy settled into bed and making sure she was all right.

"Looks like you got yourself a woman." Maverick's voice held all kinds of questions.

Tanner wasn't sure how to explain his relationship with Maisy to everyone when he couldn't even explain it to himself.

Before he could think of something, the cabin door opened and Clementine stepped out onto the raised porch, wiping her hands on her apron. Her wavy blond-red hair was looped up into a messy bun with loose strands framing her face.

Of all the Oakley siblings, he'd always predicted that Clementine would get married first. She was the most outgoing and vivacious of all of them, and she was one of the most beautiful women in the high country.

But here she was, recently having turned twenty, still single and still living on the ranch. And as far as Tanner knew, she didn't have a steady beau, although she could have any fellow she wanted if she snapped her fingers at one.

Tanner wasn't sure what was holding Clementine back from getting into a relationship. Even though she was busy with her candy-making endeavors and hoped to open her own shop someday, that wasn't enough to keep her from finding love.

Clementine claimed that she'd fallen for Franz when he'd arrived earlier in the year and that she'd never recovered from him choosing her twin sister Clarabelle over her. But Tanner suspected Clementine's hesitancies went deeper than a love triangle gone awry.

Whatever the case, Clementine was always helpful and sweet and cheerful whenever he was home. Now, as she came forward with a smile, she stopped short at the sight of Maisy on his lap, her mouth open, her greeting forgotten.

It was bad enough having to explain Maisy's presence to Maverick, who was a little dense when it came to the ways of love. But Clementine? She was savvy and would scrutinize him and Maisy and figure out something was going on between them.

The lack of motion of the horse seemed to alert Maisy to a change, and she stirred against him. Without opening her eyes, she glided her hand up his chest again to his neck. "Have you kissed me yet?" Her words were somewhat slurred, but still clear enough, at least to him.

From the way Maverick's footsteps stopped short a dozen paces away and Clementine's eyes widened, he guessed Maisy's question hadn't been lost on them either.

"Now, darlin'," he said quickly, hoping the two wouldn't hear his response, "remember what I told you? We're waiting for a special occasion."

"What if I don't want to?" Her lashes lifted, and her gaze drifted up to his mouth.

At any other time, he would have interpreted her look as an invitation. And it would have sent him spiraling with desire that would have been difficult to resist. But with Maverick and Clementine both watching him with undisguised interest, his muscles tensed, especially in the back of his neck.

"I think I'd like another kiss right now." Maisy's voice

wasn't quiet or private. No doubt the entire ranch could hear her request. At the very least, Maverick and Clementine had heard. "Please, Tanner. I love your kisses." Her lashes fell to her cheeks, and she let her hand drop from his neck as she leaned her head against his chest.

He wanted to knead the back of his neck and work out the ever-tightening kink. But his arms were full of Maisy, and even though he was embarrassed by the situation, he wouldn't ever do anything that would cause her harm.

"So . . ." Maverick's grin was widening. "Should we go away for a minute so you can get to it?"

Tanner tossed Maverick a glare before glancing down at Maisy to gauge her reaction to Maverick's comment. Her eyes remained closed, and she leaned against him heavily, as if she'd gone back to sleep.

Clementine had moved to the edge of the porch railing, and she was taking in Maisy's position on his lap, no doubt noticing the protective way he was holding her, as if she were a priceless treasure.

She *was* a priceless treasure, worth more to him than anything else. That was the truth, and there was no sense in denying it. But that didn't mean he had any right to the treasure—not when he couldn't promise to value her the way she deserved.

"Well, Tanner Oakley," Clementine said, her smile

now growing too. "Looks like you've finally found the love of your life."

The love of his life. Was that the description he'd been fumbling to find?

As his arms tightened around her, he realized with a clarity that had eluded him so far that, yes, Maisy was the love of his life. He loved her more than he loved anyone else—even Ryder. In fact, he loved her so much that he was willing to sacrifice everything—even his own happiness in being with her—so that he could send her away and she could have the kind of life she'd dreamed of.

That was the simple truth.

An ache began to pulse in his chest.

"Tanner's in love." Maverick's tone held a note of both teasing and awe.

Tanner wasn't ready to admit it to Maverick and Clementine, but he didn't deny their statements either. "Maisy's been shot. Dr. Howell did surgery last night to remove the bullet, and he's fixed her up as best as he could. And now I need a place where she can recuperate."

"Shot?" Clementine's brows furrowed with sudden concern, and she started down the steps toward him. "How?"

As Maverick and Clementine helped him lift Maisy out of the saddle and carry her into the house, he explained the conflict that had escalated with her neighbor over her wolf. He warned Maverick that Smoke had followed Maisy down from the mountains and was probably nearby, although he hadn't seen the wolf yet today.

They placed Maisy in the bed in Tanner's old room—the room he'd once shared with Ryder and that he now stayed in whenever he visited the ranch. One of his recent journals was tucked under the bed where he'd left it, but otherwise the room was sparsely furnished, since neither he nor Ryder had ever owned much.

Thankfully, Maisy didn't awaken again during the carrying inside. Even if he could admit to himself that he loved her, he didn't want any more questions from his family. And they were sure to ask him more—and tease him more—if Maisy mentioned kissing him again.

Clementine lifted Maisy's head and slipped a pillow underneath. Then she smoothed Maisy's hair back. As she did so, she straightened, her expression radiating alarm. "Maisy's burning up."

Maverick had left to retrieve their bags from the gelding. Tanner, in the process of unfolding another blanket to drape across Maisy, halted and scanned her face. Her cheeks were rosy, and her forehead was now damp, with strands of hair sticking to her skin.

He placed a hand across her forehead, and sure enough, her skin was hot to the touch. He didn't have to ask Clementine what it meant. He already knew. Maisy wasn't getting better.

She was worse.

16

Maisy couldn't keep from screaming. The burning in her shoulder felt as though someone was thrusting a cattle branding iron deep into her flesh and torturing her.

Every time she awoke to her own screaming, Tanner was at her side, his handsome face hovering above her as he pressed a cool cloth against her hot face and neck.

Even in her delirious state, she could see the worry in his eyes and knew she wasn't doing well.

She couldn't tell where she was, although she had vague recollections of riding a horse away from her mountain cabin and arriving at a doctor's office someplace. But the memories were scattered, and she wasn't sure what was real anymore.

Had she gotten shot trying to save Smoke? And had Tanner brought her down the mountain? Was he really with her? Or was she only dreaming everything?

A few times when she thrashed about, a young

woman was also there, bending over her with compassionate green eyes and a forehead furrowed with anxiety. Another time or two, she thought she saw an older man's face, perhaps the doctor.

But mostly she saw Tanner. And whenever he wasn't there, she cried out for him. She wasn't sure why she needed him so much, but he was the only one she wanted.

As she regained consciousness after what seemed an eternity of suffering, her fingers pressed against the cool sheets beneath her. She could feel that she was in a bed, although from the firmness of the mattress, she knew it wasn't the one in the cabin.

In an instant, she sensed that the burning in her body was gone. All that was left was a low throbbing in her shoulder.

Her eyes flew open to reveal a room she'd never been in before—one with log walls and low rafters. Natural light filtered through a single window framed by simple blue curtains, and she guessed the day was cloudy or that it was almost evening.

At the scratching of what sounded like pen against paper, she shifted and saw Tanner sitting in a chair beside the bed with a journal open on his lap. He was busy writing, his focus on the paper, his mind clearly filled with whatever thoughts he was bringing to life.

He was wearing a blue wool shirt—one she hadn't

seen on him before but that brought out the life and energy in his face, highlighting the angular lines of his jaw and cheeks. Although his face was still covered in a layer of scruff, it wasn't quite as thick as it had been previously. His hair was mussed, but it looked freshly washed.

She glanced around the room again, searching for some sign of where they were. It was a small but clean room, and the scent of something freshly baked and sweet wafted in the air, making her stomach rumble.

How long had it been since she'd eaten?

As though he'd heard her question, or at least heard her stomach's complaint, his gaze darted to her.

At the sight of her eyes open, he startled, dropped his pen, and fumbled with his journal. "You're awake."

"Yes, it looks that way." Her voice came out scratchy. "I reckon I wouldn't be this hungry if I were just dreaming."

"You're hungry?" He sat forward, scanning her face and then her shoulder.

She started to push herself up and only then realized her shoulder was bare except for a loose bandage covering her. She also seemed to be wearing a thin nightgown, but it was only partially covering her body so that her injury was easy to access.

As the sheet on top fell away, too late she realized just how indecent she was. Before the sheet could slip farther down, she clutched it and flattened herself to the mattress and mound of pillows behind her.

Thankfully, Tanner didn't seem to be paying attention to her state of undress and was instead setting aside his journal and standing. "Is your fever finally gone?"

"I think so." She cupped one of her hands to her forehead. Her skin felt cool and clammy.

"Thank the Lord in heaven above." His eyes rapidly turned glossy, and he pivoted away and pressed his thumbs to his eyes.

"Was I that bad?" She'd never seen Tanner so emotional before.

He nodded but didn't speak.

"Close to dying?"

He nodded again.

Though she felt weak, she didn't feel sick. "How long did I have the fever?"

Drawing in a breath, he turned back around, his expression composed but grave. "We've been here about a week."

She'd been battling a fever for a week?

"The gunshot wound festered pretty badly." He nodded toward the bedside table that was filled with bottles of medicine of every shape and size. "But the doctor had all the right medicines. And then, of course, Clementine found some of our ma's herbal remedies and applied those."

Maisy took in the room again. "Does that mean we're at your family's ranch?"

"Yes."

Her mind was fuzzy on the details of all that had happened, as though she was wading through thick fog to find the answers, especially how she'd gotten there.

Tanner stepped closer and laid a hand on her forehead.

His touch was cool and gentle, and she loved it, as always. But even as she was tempted to lean into his touch, she paused. Something had happened between them to push them apart. What was it?

"The fever *is* gone." His voice filled with relief.

"Didn't believe I could tell the difference between hot and cold?" she teased.

"Didn't believe you were really awake." His lips formed into one of his charming grins—one that curled his upper lip in that adorable way that made her want to kiss it.

Kiss him? What was she thinking?

His eyes took on the twinkle that she loved. "There were a couple of times you awoke and said some interesting things."

"Like what?"

His gaze shifted to her mouth before darting away and looking everywhere but at her.

It was something embarrassing. "C'mon, big guy. Just tell me."

He shook his head, his brown eyes as rich and warm and kind as always. "I'll go get you something to eat."

"Not till you tell me what I said."

He shrugged as if he'd tried to warn her. "It was about kissing."

"What did I say?"

His grin inched up again. "You sure you want to hear?"

She tried to swat him playfully, but she could hardly lift her arm, grimacing instead at the pain the slight movement caused.

"Take it easy, darlin'."

"Tell me," she demanded.

"You bossed me around for a kiss."

He couldn't be serious. "I did not."

"You did." He tilted his head almost arrogantly. "In fact, you told everyone just how much you *love* my kisses."

"Hush up." Her mind scrambled for some memory, and she had the vague feeling she'd been sitting on Tanner's lap and *had* been talking about kissing him. "Who heard me say it?"

"Maverick and Clementine." Tanner's eyes were filled with mirth.

Fresh heat splashed through her, this time from embarrassment. "I was delusional. That's all. And I didn't mean one lick of what I said."

He chuckled softly. "I think you meant every word."

She tried to reach for her pillow to toss at him, but she only managed to pull it out part way before she was breathing hard.

"Hey, now." Tanner's humor disappeared as he adjusted the pillow back under her head. "No pillow fights today."

A sense of exhaustion was already beginning to press through her. She didn't understand how she could be so tired after having been in bed all week, but after being close to death, it would probably take time before she was feeling back to normal.

After situating her, Tanner left the room, making her promise to stay awake until he returned with something to eat. Once he was gone, unease sifted through her. Something wasn't right. Even though they'd bantered like they always had, Tanner wasn't himself, as though a wall had gone up between them.

She closed her eyes and quieted her thoughts, turning them back to the last memory she had of the cabin. She'd gone after help for Nelly and had fallen from the trail onto a ledge. Smoke had gone off and returned with Tanner.

Smoke.

Maisy sat up so abruptly that the bandage fell from her wound. The sheet started to slip down too, but she clutched it and brought it up to her chin.

The memories of the last night in the cabin came rushing back—how she'd kissed Tanner and told him she might be falling in love with him. But he'd disregarded the kiss and her love in one easy move when he'd unholstered his gun and almost shot Smoke.

All the humor and relief from moments ago fled from her heart as if fleeing from an impending storm. A cold emptiness filled her instead.

Tanner had rejected her offer of love and a life together. Even more than simply rejecting her offer, he'd tried to sabotage their relationship by killing Smoke. She knew with certainty that was why he'd broken the kiss and aimed his gun at the wolf—because in doing so, he knew that she'd end up hating him. And in hating him, she'd be able to let him go.

He could have just told her he didn't want to be with her, that he didn't foresee a future together.

But if he'd admitted it, would she have listened, especially since he'd already hinted that was how he felt? With how stubborn she was, she probably would have kept pestering him until he gave in to her and relinquished all his plans in order to be with her. And that wasn't how she wanted to win him over.

She wanted a man to love her freely enough that he wouldn't care where he was or what he was doing as long as he was with her.

But Tanner didn't want to give her that kind of love.

He'd made that clear enough at the cabin.

She lowered herself back to the pillows and closed her eyes tightly, squeezing back sudden hot tears. The problem was, she didn't hate him for what had happened with Smoke. She could never hate him.

But she was angry at him for making her fall in love with him and then not wanting her. It was an irrational anger, she knew. But the frustration swirled inside anyway.

And disappointment. Mostly at herself for being so weak. She'd watched the way her ma and Nelly had struggled in their marriages—the loneliness, heartache, and difficulties. She'd told herself she wouldn't settle for the same kind of life they'd had, that she wanted more.

But after less than a week with Tanner and a few kisses, she'd been willing and ready to throw away all her plans to be with him. Even though she'd tried hard to keep from being like Ma and Nelly, maybe she wasn't so different after all.

Confound it all. She couldn't forget all that Ma and Nelly had suffered, and she had to stop letting herself care about Tanner—had to cut her feelings off and move forward without him.

It was the only way.

"Clementine baked some sweet rolls." Tanner's voice came from the doorway, full of life and enthusiasm. "And I have a cup of freshly brewed coffee."

She rolled so that she was facing away from him, her eyes still closed. "I'm not hungry anymore."

Partway across the room, Tanner's footsteps halted. He stood quietly, likely watching her and trying to make sense of her abrupt mood change.

She probably should just talk to him and tell him everything she was feeling. But hadn't she already tried to have a conversation at the cabin about them and the changing nature of their relationship? He'd made his position clear, and now it was time for her to do the same.

After a moment, his footsteps continued to the bed, stopping behind her. "I guess you remembered everything that happened at the cabin."

"Yep. And the less we say to each other, the better."

He was silent for a beat. "I regret how I handled everything. I was a fool, and I apologize—"

"Fine. I accept your apology, but that doesn't mean I want to be friends anymore."

"I'm sorry I hurt you." His voice held remorse. "But I want to make it up to you."

"Nope. What happened was for the best. It reminded me of why we could never work out and why I can't give up the future I want."

He didn't respond.

"You were right." She forced the words she knew she needed to say. "You're no good for me, and I can't change my plans for you."

The words sounded as harsh this time as they had when he'd spoken them, but she had to force herself to accept the truth. And she had to make sure he understood that she wasn't letting herself be swept away by his charm any longer.

He sighed, then waited for several moments, as if he expected her to say more.

But she'd done enough to make a fool of herself over him, and now she had to muster up self-respect and self-preservation. The best thing was to cut him out of her life.

"I'll leave this food here for you."

"Fine. Thank you."

She could hear him moving aside medicine bottles and setting dishes on the bedside table. When he finished, he waited another minute.

Her muscles tensed with the need for him to reassure her that everything would be okay between them. But even as the longing swelled deep inside, she forced it back down. Although it would be painful, she had to break the connection. Then she could finally prove to herself that she was a stronger and better woman than her ma.

She clamped her lips together and didn't move.

A few seconds later, his footsteps continued across the room and out the door. As soon as the steps began to recede down the hallway, she let out a breath.

Hot tears slipped from her eyes even though she had them squeezed shut. She swiped them away and tried to make herself angry at Tanner again. But the longing inside was still too strong, and she suspected it would be until she was far away from him.

That meant she had to get better and leave just as soon as she could.

Maisy's silence was more than he could bear.

Tanner sat forward in the chair beside her bed. His journal was open, but his pen was idle on the blank page. He'd been trying to write a little bit each day about the recent events up in the mountains with Lester and Smoke and Maisy, but every time he started penning the story, he couldn't keep the sadness at bay—sadness that those days with her had been so fleeting.

And sadness because after she'd awoken yesterday, she'd been so cold with him. He knew it was just with him, because she was talkative with Clementine, Hazel, and Maverick whenever they visited her.

She'd even been chatty with the doctor when he'd come this morning to check on her. Although her wound was still tender, the doctor had taken one look at it and declared she was on the mend. When she'd asked how much longer she would need to be abed, he'd said that if she was a good girl and rested a lot, it might only be a few more days.

Apparently she was in a hurry to get out of bed—likely to get away from him—because she was taking the doctor's orders to rest seriously. At least, she was resting whenever he was in the room with her.

He didn't know how much longer he could let the tension stretch before apologizing again. But after apologizing multiple times now, it was clear the tactic wasn't working.

Should he just blurt out that he loved her? Would that make everything better? It wouldn't hurt to try, would it? Because the truth was, over the past week of watching her hover between life and death, he'd realized all the more clearly just how much he loved her and didn't want to let her go. At the prospect of having to live without her, his life stretched out bleakly in front of him. If he'd thought he'd been lost and without any ties before, this was worse.

At the same time, her words from yesterday had plagued him too: *"What happened was for the best. It reminded me of why we could never work out and why I can't give up the future I want."*

That was one of the reasons he'd resisted a relationship with her all along—because he wanted her to be free to live a different life from everything she'd ever known, a life that was stable and secure and happy. And that kind of life didn't involve her remaining in the area and being tied to a mountain man like him.

But what if he gave up his mountain-man ways and settled down? Last night he'd even talked with Maverick about the possibility of taking over Ryder's ranch near Frisco. If he had land in the valley, a home, steady work, and goals for his life, would that be enough for her? Would that fulfill her dreams of what she wanted in a husband?

The trouble was, even if he could temporarily fulfill her dreams, what happened when he got tired of living on the ranch and was ready to move on? He refused to think of leaving a wife and family behind. But he also couldn't ask her to give up a normal life to move around with him. Would they both end up miserable?

With a heavy sigh, he sank back into the chair again and picked up the pen. He peered out the window to the hills in the distance. The midday sunshine had made an appearance, but now in late October, it had lost its warmth and brilliance. Even so, it highlighted a lone creature sitting atop a rocky outcropping overlooking the ranch.

It was Smoke. The wolf had been lingering on the outskirts of the ranch all week. In the few moments Tanner had taken a break from sitting beside Maisy, he'd gone out and hunted game for the wolf, leaving an elk carcass one day and a hare another. He'd hoped the offerings would keep Smoke from drawing too near the cattle or horses. Even though he'd asked Maverick and the other ranch hands not to shoot at Smoke, the wolf was still in danger. No one in his right mind would hesitate to kill the creature if he came near the livestock.

If they moved to Ryder's ranch, Smoke would have a better chance of surviving.

Tanner stared at the empty page, twisted his pen around his fingers, then snapped the book closed and stared at the outline of Maisy beneath the covers.

The problem was, even if he made a case for the move, she was still too mad to consider the option.

She sighed, although it was so quiet he couldn't be sure.

One thing *was* sure, though. He couldn't go on this way with the unending silence between them. "Maisy?" he said softly. "We need to talk."

She didn't say anything back.

"Please?"

This time her sigh was loud and exasperated.

Before he could formulate any words, horse hooves pounded through the ranch yard, loudly and urgently enough that he stood. Since the window faced the backyard, he wasn't able to see who the newcomer was.

But a few seconds later, shouts filled the air, followed by heavy bootsteps thudding up the porch stairs. Clementine wasn't home—had gone to town hours ago to help in Worth's General Store, where she sold her candy.

Maisy rolled over, wincing with the movement. Her face was pale from the days of lying near death's door, and her blue-green eyes looked especially bright.

Loud banging resounded against the front door. "Open up, Tanner!" came a man's gruff shout.

"Who in the blazes?" Tanner unholstered his revolver.

"It's Pa." Maisy tried pushing herself up but only made it halfway.

"I know you're in there with my daughter!" Sure enough, the bellow belonged to Cleveland Merritt.

As Tanner stepped into the wide front room of the house, which contained several sofas centered around a large fireplace, he stuffed his revolver away and tried to tamp down his irritation at Maisy's pa for finally coming to look for her.

Before he could make it past the first sofa, the lock popped off the inside and the door flew open.

Cleveland burst inside and barreled forward, his burly body twice the size of a normal man's—even more so with the bearskin robe he was wearing over his garments. His black curly hair was long and pulled back into a leather strap beneath a coonskin cap similar to the one Tanner wore. And his weathered face was barely visible beneath the layer of scruff and his curly black beard.

His dark eyes locked on Tanner and his nostrils flared

like a bull about to charge. "Tanner Oakley! You're a dead man!"

Dead man?

Tanner halted, unable to comprehend Cleveland's threat. Why was the fellow angry with him? Especially after he'd brought Maisy to town and saved her life.

Maybe Cleveland had heard about the gun battle over Smoke from Lester and was mad that Tanner hadn't done more to protect Maisy and see that she didn't get herself into the predicament to begin with. Tanner had beaten himself up over the incident plenty of times already and didn't need Cleveland heaping guilt upon him.

Or what if Cleveland was just as angry as Lester had predicted about Tanner living at the cabin with Maisy? Yes, that had to be it. All Tanner needed to do was explain the truth and make Cleveland see reason.

"Hold on now." Tanner put out a hand to stop the man's approach.

But Cleveland's stride didn't falter and neither did his fierce scowl. He stomped forward as though he planned to trample Tanner into dust.

Tanner squared his shoulders. "Don't worry. Maisy's alive and recovering just fine."

"Yep, already been to the doc in town and heard she'll live." Cleveland's steps clobbered ominously. "But that ain't gonna stop me from carving up your pretty face!"

Only then did Tanner notice Cleveland had

unsheathed his hunting knife, a weapon that had a seven-inch blade sharp enough to slice through tough animal hide and bone. Tanner stumbled back a step and reached again for his revolver, but the man was already lunging for Tanner, grabbing his arm and twisting it hard behind his back.

With his free hand, Tanner slipped his gun out and had it ready to shoot in an instant. And even though he could have put a bullet in the big fellow's foot to stop him, Tanner knew he'd never be able to pull the trigger and bring harm to Maisy's pa. If he did so, she would never forgive him, and he'd never be able to forgive himself.

He had to solve this dispute with Cleveland without bloodshed.

Tanner stuffed his revolver away. He was strong and could fight against the brawniest of men. He'd had to at times, with the rough crowd that lived in the high altitudes. With a grunt, he reached up to wrap an arm around Cleveland and put him in a chokehold. But in the next instant, the hunting blade cut into Tanner's neck with a sting that brought him to a standstill.

"You're a dead man, Tanner. A dead man, y'hear?" Cleveland stank of bear grease and woodsmoke. At this proximity, Tanner could smell his breath too, which reeked of garlic and tobacco.

"Pa, that's enough." Maisy stood in the bedroom

doorway, clutching the frame and leaning against it, breathless and flushed. Her hair was loose and fell down to her waist, and she'd wrapped a blanket around herself. But that didn't conceal her nightgown or the way it slipped off her injured shoulder, exposing a patch of skin from her neck to her arm.

It was a smooth, beautiful stretch, pale and dotted with freckles. And it was bare.

"Keep your eyes off her!" Cleveland roared, jerking Tanner backward. "Or I'll cut your eyeballs out first." With the threat hanging in the air, Cleveland shifted the knife from Tanner's neck to his cheek, just below one of his eyes, so that the pointed blade bit into Tanner's skin.

"Pa!" Maisy shouted with a glare at her father. "Stop hurting Tanner."

"Don't you sass me, girlie." Cleveland kept the knife right where it was.

A warm trickle of blood dribbled down Tanner's face.

Tanner held himself absolutely still. Maybe he should have shot Cleveland after all. The fellow was acting like a mad dog.

"What's going on?" Maverick barged through the front door, breathing hard, his rifle in hand. One of his ranch hands halted behind him, also carrying a rifle.

At the sight of Cleveland's knife against Tanner's face, Maverick's expression hardened.

Cleveland didn't seem at all bothered by the

appearance of two men pointing guns at him. Instead, he leveled another fierce look at Tanner. "I've come to cut up this here boy for defiling my little baby girl."

"That never happened," Tanner rushed to explain, even as he realized he had his gun out again.

"Ain't nobody defiled Maisy." Maverick was aiming his rifle at Cleveland's head.

Tanner's gut clenched with sudden fear that the situation could easily go from bad to worse in a few seconds. He knew that all too well from everything that had happened at the cabin when Maisy had been shot.

"Listen." Tanner tried to keep his voice calm and level as he slipped his revolver away. "Let's all put the weapons down so no one gets hurt."

Cleveland pinched Tanner's arm behind his back. "Oh, you're getting hurt all right. I'm gonna slice you up until you're bleeding all over the floor."

"Pa!" Maisy pushed away from the door and took halting steps toward the burly man in his bearskin coat. "Lester Acker's been feeding you lies. Tanner didn't defile me."

"Oh yes he did!" Cleveland's roar was like that of an angry bear defending a cub.

Maisy didn't miss a beat as she neared him, not in the least intimidated by the bluster. "Tanner helped me, that's all."

"He *helped himself* to having what wasn't his—"

"That's not true." Maisy's eyes were blazing as she halted in front of Tanner and grabbed for her pa's hand holding the knife as though she meant to disarm him. How she would manage such a feat, Tanner didn't know. But he wasn't surprised Maisy thought she could.

Cleveland moved the knife high in the air out of her reach, and Tanner breathed a little easier without it pricking his face. Even though he didn't think Cleveland would follow through on his threat to cut him up, he'd also never seen the fellow so mad.

Maisy clawed at her pa's arm, going after the knife again, but then halted with a wince, clearly doing too much and risking opening her shoulder wound.

"Maisy," Tanner warned, unable to hold himself back. "You're overdoing it."

She only shot him a glare too, reminding him they weren't exactly on the best of terms. Then she shoved her pa. "Let him go. You know Tanner's an honorable man."

Cleveland's brows furrowed deeply above his dark eyes as he peered down at his daughter. "Heard from multiple people that Tanner was holed up with you for the past couple weeks and taking what don't belong to him."

"He stayed with me less than a week. And he wasn't taking anything."

"Oh, he was taking all right." Cleveland jerked on Tanner's arm that was twisted behind his back, this time hard enough to make Tanner grimace. "Weren't you, pretty boy?"

"No." Even as Tanner denied Cleveland's accusation, a needle of guilt kept him from saying more.

"So you're telling me you never once touched my baby girl?"

Tanner pressed his lips together, guessing it was better if he didn't say anything at all.

But Maisy huffed. "A little kissing never hurt anyone."

Tanner almost groaned at her confession, but before he could, Cleveland was roaring in anger and dropped the knife back against Tanner's throat, hard enough to draw blood again.

Maisy screamed, her eyes riveted to the knife and turning wild.

"Now hold on!" Maverick yelled, stepping farther into the room, his rifle still aimed at Cleveland's head, his finger on the trigger.

The situation was escalating too quickly. "Stop!" Tanner shouted. "I don't want Maisy getting hurt again!"

Cleveland released the pressure of the knife on Tanner's throat but still kept his hold on Tanner. "I won't be putting my knife away—not until the preacher pronounces you man and wife."

At the ultimatum, Maisy took a rapid step back. "I'm not marrying Tanner."

Cleveland leveled a withering look on her. "Oh yes you are, girlie."

What was Cleveland saying? That he intended to force a wedding?

Tanner's mind was spinning. Could he really marry Maisy? He loved her. And hadn't he just considered giving up his mountain-man ways in order to settle down on Ryder's ranch?

"Yep." Maverick inched closer. "I think that's a good idea. Tanner should marry Maisy."

Tanner knew he should argue against his brother and her pa, but he couldn't muster enough opposition to the idea of marrying her to put up more of a fight.

Cleveland gave a sharp nod. "Course it's a good idea. It's the only way to save her reputation."

"I don't care about my reputation here." Maisy pressed against the wall as though she needed the support. Her eyes were round, and Tanner was afraid she would collapse.

"You need to get back in bed, Maisy," he urged her gently. "You're still too weak to be up and about."

"I'm fine." Her eyes flashed with frustration. "Or at least, I'll be fine enough once everyone puts the idea of marriage out of their heads, because it's not gonna happen."

"Oh, you bet it's happening." Cleveland guffawed and then turned and called across the room and out the open door. "Glenn?"

A second man in a coonskin cap poked his head into the cabin. It was Glenn, who was just as scraggly looking as Cleveland with his long greasy hair and overgrown beard. But where Cleveland was big and burly, Glenn was thin and lanky, his limbs like twigs. He swept his gaze over the room, taking in everyone before nodding at Cleveland. "You ready?"

"More than ready," Cleveland boomed.

With the tip of his rifle, Glenn nudged another fellow into the house. Reverend Livingston. In a dark suit and wearing a clerical collar, the man edged forward reluctantly, his kindly eyes wary. He was a short waif of a man who could be easily trampled by either Cleveland or Glenn.

"Pa!" Maisy bunched her hands on her hips. "You didn't force the reverend to come out, did you?"

"Of course I did!"

Tanner tossed what he hoped was an apologetic look the reverend's way. Maverick had already crossed toward Glenn and pushed the fellow's rifle away from the reverend.

"Get over here, Reverend, and get this ceremony going," Cleveland called. "Before I cut him up some more."

Cleveland jabbed his knife against Tanner's face again, this time with the blade at his chin.

The reverend blanched, likely taking in the size of the knife and perhaps the blood that coated Tanner's cheek and neck. It probably looked worse than it was. Even so, the reverend scurried forward while opening his prayer book.

Tanner inwardly sighed. Cleveland Merritt intended to make him marry Maisy today and wasn't going to take no for an answer. The trouble was, Maisy's stormy expression said clearly enough that she wasn't planning to say yes—at least, not without a fight.

"Nope," Maisy stated again, this time more emphatically. "I'm not getting married today, and that's all there is to it."

It was already bad enough that she was here with Tanner at his family's ranch and imposing on him while she recovered from her gunshot wound. She'd been working up a way to tell him today that he needed to go back to the mountains and leave her to recuperate on her own.

It was past time for them to go their separate ways. But she hadn't exactly been sure how to say that since it was his family's house and she was the guest there.

Pa sidled toward her, dragging Tanner along with him. He nodded at the reverend. "Come on over here, Reverend."

Reverend Livingston was quickly flipping through his prayer book, glancing from Glenn to her pa and back as if he was afraid he might get shot if he didn't cooperate fast enough. And now he shuffled closer to her as Pa positioned Tanner beside her.

Tanner had lifted his chin to keep the blade of the knife from puncturing his skin, but it was already nicked and bleeding.

"Go ahead, Reverend," Pa said loudly before clearing his throat and speaking in a normal tone. "And thank you kindly for your services."

The reverend stood in front of her and Tanner, and as he flattened the open page of the prayer book, he glanced at Tanner, then grimaced at the new trail of blood on his chin. "Is the knife necessary, Mr. Merritt?"

Cleveland glowered at Tanner. "I won't be moving my knife until this fella does the right thing for my baby girl and gives her his name."

"You're being a little—a lot—extreme." Maisy leaned more heavily against the door frame, her legs weaker than she'd expected for the first time being out of bed in over a week.

Tanner reached out a hand, but before he could lend her support, Pa jerked his arm behind his back. "You better not touch her again until she's your wife."

"That's enough!" She had to put an end to her pa's shenanigans. "You can't do this, Pa. You can't make me and Tanner get married."

He jutted his chin, his dark eyes filled with

stubbornness. "Watch me."

She jutted her chin too. "Just as soon as I'm healed up, I'm going to go to Minnesota and live with Ma's family, her sister."

Pa shook his head curtly. "She's dead."

Maisy's heart dropped. "You're just saying that because you don't want me to go."

"She passed away shortly after your ma did, and her one son who wrote to me said he was heading to California."

Something in Pa's tone told her he was telling the truth.

She couldn't keep her shoulders from drooping right along with her heart. So much for leaving and starting a normal life someplace new. What would she do now? Where could she go?

Pa narrowed his eyes and locked gazes with her. "Best thing is for you to get married."

She didn't look away. She'd never let him intimidate her before, and she wouldn't start now.

The room around them grew quiet.

A gravity settled over her pa's expression. "I mean it, Maisy. Much as I like Tanner, I'll kill him before I let him walk away from you."

Was he really serious? An anxious tremor pulsed through her stomach. He couldn't really be thinking about killing Tanner, could he?

"Could I talk to Maisy privately?" Tanner held his chin high to keep the blade from going too deep.

"Nope. Ain't lettin' you plot with her how to put an end to the marriage before it has a chance to begin."

If they went through with the ceremony to appease Pa, could they get an annulment later and go their separate ways?

Tanner gulped, his Adam's apple sliding up and down prominently. "I wasn't planning to plot how to end it. Just wanted to reassure her."

"That so?" Pa's brows shot up. "Then go right ahead here in front of us all."

Maisy finally met Tanner's gaze to find him silently communicating with her that everything would be all right.

"Go on." Pa gave Tanner a slight shove.

She sighed. Pa was overbearing at times, and this was one of those times.

"Listen, Maisy." Tanner's voice was filled with a strange earnestness. "We don't need to have it all figured out. So long as we care about each other, we can make it work, can't we?"

Could they? Hadn't that been the problem all along with them? Yep, they cared about each other. Even if Tanner hadn't reciprocated telling her he loved her that night at the cabin, she knew he still cared and had proven it over the past week by saving her. But they both wanted different things from life and couldn't reconcile those differences. How would marriage make it any easier? Wouldn't it only make the issues worse?

Maybe if she stalled, everyone would go away. Or at the very least, she could come up with a better plan now that she couldn't travel to Minnesota.

"Can I have some time to think about it?" she finally asked, directing her question at Pa.

Pa shook his head, then glanced at Glenn, who was waiting inside the open door with two of Maverick's ranch hands. Glenn gave him a nod, as though to encourage him to continue.

Pa drew in a breath. "It's like this, girlie. Me and Glenn have been considering moving on up to Wyoming before winter settles in, since the hunting is better there this year. But we didn't think we could with the womenfolk and a new babe."

That news didn't surprise her. Pa had been talking about moving for a while now.

Before she could say anything, he continued. "When we got back a few days ago and heard Nelly and the baby were gone, we reckoned we still might have the chance of moving if we acted right away."

Her heartbeat pattered nearly to a halt.

"If we get you married quick-like, then we don't have to worry about dragging you along and having you slow us down."

So, that was it. The real reason Pa wanted her to marry Tanner. Because he wanted to be rid of her and have the freedom he needed to go wherever and do whatever he wanted.

A shaft of pain pricked at her already sore heart. Sure, Pa cared about her reputation and her well-being. And he was mad about Tanner staying at the cabin. But more than that, he cared about his own life and being his own man. Just as he always had.

She was a nuisance to him, a burden, an inconvenience. And he wanted to leave her again. This time for good.

Well, let him. "Fine." She grabbed Tanner's arm. "Let's get married."

With the knife still pressed to his chin, Tanner slid an arm around her waist and braced her up, not seeming to care that with each movement he was bleeding more. "Are you sure?" he asked softly. "We don't have to—"

"I want to." *Want* wasn't the right word. But marriage was the quickest and easiest way to give her pa his freedom. In fact, if she didn't marry Tanner, her pa would just foist her off onto some other fellow in the area since he was so confounded determined to be rid of her. And if she had to get married, it might as well be to Tanner.

She could feel Tanner watching her, trying to figure out why she'd changed her mind so quickly. But she wasn't in the mood to explain anything. The sooner she and Tanner were married, the sooner Pa and Glenn could move on and she wouldn't have to hold them back anymore. Then maybe she'd never have to see either one ever again.

She grabbed her pa's hand and pinched it hard to make him stop hurting Tanner. All the while, she refused to meet his gaze, not wanting to give him the satisfaction of seeing the apology sure to be in his eyes.

He held the knife against Tanner another moment before finally lowering and sheathing it. With the knife gone, she suddenly felt weak and alone and helpless.

Tanner stepped closer to her, bracing her up even more. And even though she wanted to push him away and stand up on her own two feet, she let herself lean against him. She didn't want to need Tanner, didn't want to rely on him, didn't want to trust him. But in the moment, she knew she couldn't stand on her own two feet and make it by herself. He was all she had, and without him, she'd surely fall.

"Go ahead, Reverend," she said before Pa could order the kindly man around any further.

Within minutes, Reverend Livingston was leading them through their vows and Tanner was slipping a ring on her finger—one that had belonged first to her ma and then to Nelly and now would be hers. She didn't want to think about how she was marrying a mountain man too, even though she'd never wanted to.

The reverend read the final lines of the wedding ceremony: "For as much as Tanner and Maisy have consented together in holy wedlock and have witnessed the same before God and this company, and thereto have given and pledged their troth each to the other and have declared the same by giving and receiving of a ring and by joining of hands, I pronounce that they be man and wife together. In the name of the Father, of the Son, and of the Holy Ghost."

She blinked back tears. She wasn't sure what the tears meant, but she did know they weren't from happiness.

At the reverend's last word, she released Tanner. She could feel his intense gaze upon her, just as she had during the whole ceremony, seeming to ask her if she was okay.

She didn't want to answer his question. All she wanted to do was escape.

Before anyone could talk to her, she turned into the bedroom and closed the door, blocking out everyone.

She leaned back against the door and pressed a hand to her chest, which ached more than her shoulder. Even though she tried to hold back the tears, they came anyway, coursing down her cheeks.

"Maisy?" Pa called from the other side of the door.

She didn't answer.

"I'm leaving." He waited for a long moment, as though expecting her to reply. But she didn't want to say goodbye, because maybe then his leaving her behind wouldn't feel so final.

"Take care of yourself, girlie." His words were soft and only made the tears fall faster.

His footsteps thudded away, and his boisterous voice rang out as he called his goodbyes to everyone else.

She didn't move from the door until she was sure he was outside the house. Only then did she cross to the bed, climb under the covers, and bury her face into the pillow, letting her tears flow unchecked.

When the door opened a minute later, she guessed Tanner was checking on her. She grew motionless, not ready to face him yet and hoping he'd assume she was asleep.

She wasn't mad at him anymore or annoyed or even irritated. Nope, he'd been more than kind to her throughout the whole ordeal. In fact, he'd been kind to her from the beginning by coming to the cabin, rescuing her, and staying to help her.

She'd been the one to make a mess of things with their relationship. And now she was totally at fault for their current predicament—a forced and unwanted marriage.

As much as she cared about Tanner Oakley, she knew she couldn't stay married to him. She had to give him his freedom. Because if she didn't, sooner or later he'd end up leaving her too. Maybe she'd have to figure out a way to leave him first.

19

Tanner couldn't believe he was a married man.

Palming the back of his neck, he stared at the bedroom door, his pulse pounding. A part of him was glad Maisy was finally his and that he could stop pretending he didn't want her.

But another part of him was petrified. What if he'd made a terrible mistake? What if one or both of them ended up being unhappy? After all, they hadn't decided what they would do about their living arrangements. Where would they go? What would he do? How would they forge a life together?

At the late hour, the house was quiet behind him save for the murmur of voices and soft laughter from Hazel and Maverick, just a couple doors down from his room with Maisy.

His room with Maisy and his bed with Maisy.

Heat speared Tanner low and hard. There was no

denying that he and Maisy had plenty of mutual attraction. If their past kisses were any indication of the passion they would share, he was most definitely looking forward to gathering her in his arms again. And this time, he wouldn't have to feel any guilt. Now that they were man and wife, he'd be able to hold her and kiss her as much as he wanted.

Regardless of that marital privilege, he quickly stomped out the heat. Tonight wasn't the night to think about gathering her close. Not only was she still recovering from her gunshot wound, but they had a lot to work through before they would be ready for a real marriage.

After all, neither of them had exactly entered the union willingly. Tanner hadn't been able to think straight with Cleveland's hunting knife filleting him like a slab of buffalo meat. Hazel had since doctored his wounds, but his neck and chin still stung—the constant reminder of the sting of Cleveland's accusations about how he'd failed Maisy.

Maisy had been reluctant to marry him too. And she'd only agreed to it when Cleveland had revealed his true reason for the hasty marriage—that he'd wanted to wash his hands of his responsibility for Maisy so he could move on to a new adventure.

When Cleveland had shared his plans to move, Tanner had seen the light snuff out of Maisy's beautiful blue-green eyes. She'd been hurt that her pa had decided to leave her behind like a piece of unwanted furniture. Not that she would have wanted to go along with him anyway. But the least Cleveland could have done was express his affection for her and let her know he'd miss her and wanted to give her a better life.

Whatever the case, he wasn't joining Maisy in the bed yet. *Yet* was the key word. He had every intention of being with her eventually. Now that they were married, he would put every effort into having a good marriage like Pa and Ma Oakley's. He planned on loving her and giving her everything she wanted and needed. And he suspected she'd be just as bold with their physical relationship in marriage as she'd been during their kisses. The chemistry between them would be explosive, and he was looking forward to testing it and lighting some fuses.

But for now, he would be patient. He'd already had to use more self-control than he'd thought possible over the past two weeks with her. And he'd keep doing so as they sorted through their hurts and figured out their future.

What would they do with their future? That was the all-important question.

He paced away from the bedroom door and then back. He still didn't know how to move forward, and he'd been thinking about the options all day as he'd helped Maverick round up stray cattle. He'd hoped to keep an eye on Smoke in the process and make sure the wolf didn't get too near any of the livestock, but the creature hadn't been in sight.

Tanner had returned to check on Maisy several times throughout the day, and she'd been sleeping. He guessed the extended time out of bed, the stress of having her pa visit, and then the forced marriage had worn her out. She'd probably also needed some time alone and hadn't wanted to talk about her pa's leaving.

When Tanner had taken her a tray of supper earlier, she hadn't stirred, and he'd left it on the bedside table.

But now . . . he halted in front of the door again. Should he try to talk to her? At the very least, he could ask her how she was doing and assure her that he cared about what she was feeling.

Could they start to talk about what they would do once she was well enough to leave High C Ranch?

He'd again contemplated the possibility of contacting his brother and taking over his ranch—or at least running it while Ryder lived out East. The idea of being so tied down to one place weighed heavily upon Tanner, like an oxen yoke on his shoulders, demanding that he go one direction when he'd rather veer off wherever his feet took him from one day to the next.

But now that he was married, maybe it was time to force himself to put down roots, build a life and home, and give Maisy the normal life she wanted. Could he really do it?

Blowing out a tense breath, he opened the door and stepped into the room. It was dark, the light of the evening having faded, leaving deep shadows behind. He carefully made his way to the bedside table. Should he light the lantern? Or should they talk in the darkness? Maybe she'd feel more comfortable opening up if she didn't feel he was scrutinizing her.

He paused beside the bed. "Maisy?" He kept his voice to a whisper, not wanting to startle her.

She didn't move.

Was she ignoring him? Maybe she'd pretended to be asleep during his earlier visits so that she didn't have to interact with anyone. If that was the case, he'd given her plenty of time to herself. And now she needed a nudge to talk.

"Maisy," he said again, louder.

She still didn't respond.

His pulse picked up pace. Something wasn't right. Normally she would have answered him in her sassy voice, telling him to leave her alone or to go away or find someone else to pester.

The absolute silence was uncanny and wasn't like her.

Had her fever returned? Maybe she'd taken a turn for the worst . . .

With his heart racing, he couldn't light the bedside lantern fast enough. His fingers fumbled with the match and the glass globe until a small flame was burning and illuminating the outline of her body underneath the covers.

She hadn't moved from the last time he'd come to check on her.

"Maisy." He reached down and touched her shoulder. Except the outline was too soft.

"What in the world?" He tugged the cover away from her body to find that it wasn't her shoulder or her body. It was a mound of pillows and blankets.

He stood frozen in place. What had happened to her? Had someone taken her?

His blood chilled at the prospect, but just as quickly, he put that thought from his mind. He scanned the room to find that her bag and her belongings were all gone. She'd packed her bags and shoved the pillows and blankets under the covers as a disguise to fool him into thinking she was there. Then she'd gone out, getting a head start on wherever she'd decided to go.

His muscles tensed, and he began kneading the back of his neck again. Why? Why would she run away so soon after their wedding?

"Come on, Maisy." With the frustration mounting like a summer storm, he swiped up one of the pillows and tossed it across the room. "We could have talked first."

She'd once hinted they could have a life together, and he hadn't been open to it. Now that he was open to it, she apparently wasn't. What had changed her mind? Was she still angry with him?

Maybe. Even though she'd said she accepted his apology, that obviously hadn't resolved everything between them. She was probably still hurt and had gone along with her pa and the forced wedding to keep everyone safe, planning all along to leave him the first chance she had.

He threw another pillow. This one hit the chair, and the force toppled it backward so that it crashed against the floor.

"Blast!" The shout came out louder than he'd anticipated, but he suddenly didn't care. He didn't care about anything except her. And now she was gone.

He dropped to the edge of the bed and bowed his head, despair rushing through him in a crushing blow.

"Everything all right in there?" came Maverick's question from outside the open door of his bedroom.

"No." Nothing was all right. He was suddenly more miserable than he'd ever been in his life. The woman he loved had run off, left him, and didn't want to be with him. The empty ache in his chest swelled painfully—an empty ache that he'd tried to fill for so many years without success.

"What's going on?" Maverick asked as he hastily donned a shirt.

Tanner shook his head, trying to convince himself that he needed to send Maverick back to his wife. His relationship with Maisy wasn't anyone's problem but his, and yet he could hardly breathe.

"Where's Maisy?" Maverick approached the bed.

"She ran away." Tanner forced the words past his tight chest.

"Ran away?"

"She's gone." He wanted to storm out of the house, saddle up his horse, and track her down. He'd easily locate her within an hour. But if she didn't want to be with him, what good would it do to find her? She was stubborn and would probably figure out another way to leave him.

"You're sure she left?"

"She doesn't want me." Nobody wanted him. As soon as the words filtered through him, emptiness left a cold trail in their wake.

A faded memory took shape—one he hadn't thought about in ages, from the last orphanage he and Ryder had stayed in. It had been a hard place to live—harder than any of the others because it had been overcrowded with kids who'd been left fatherless due to the War of Rebellion. Many had previously been homeless on the streets and had become selfish and cruel in order to survive.

Ryder hadn't been afraid to stand up to anyone to protect Tanner, keeping him safe plenty of times from tormenters. Tanner had never worried about getting hurt physically, but the taunts had been relentless from one boy in particular. The day Ryder had been told he had to leave for industrial school, Tanner hadn't been able to control his tears at the prospect of losing his brother. The boy—whose name he couldn't remember anymore—had laughed at him and thrown out the words that had lingered with him for years.

"Nobody wants you," the boy had said through a gaptoothed sneer. His grimy face had been hard with a bitterness Tanner hadn't understood at the time but now guessed was a result of rejection. "Nobody wants you, not even your brother."

Even though Ryder had assured him later that he did want him and had proven it by running away with him from the orphanage so they could stay together, Tanner had felt like a burden to Ryder after that. In some ways, he'd always felt like a burden to the Oakleys too, and he supposed that had driven him out on his own just as soon as he'd been able to survive in the wilderness by himself.

Maverick stood beside him and was buttoning his shirt. "She's got a mighty big hankering for a scallywag like you." Maverick's tone was filled with a cocky confidence.

Of course Maverick, who was already married to the love of his life, would say so. "If she really wanted me, why did she leave me?"

Maverick stared hard at the bed, contemplating

Tanner's question seriously.

Tanner appreciated that he'd always been able to talk deeply with Maverick. In fact, Tanner had been the one to point out truths to Maverick when he'd been having a difficult time with Hazel before they'd gotten married. Maybe now it was Maverick's turn to point out truths to him.

Tanner waited expectantly, needing something—anything—that he could cling to.

"Both me and Hazel said the same thing," Maverick finally said quietly. "Maisy looks at you as if you're her whole world."

"I wish that was the case, but that's a stretch."

Maverick released a soft guffaw. "Reckon that girl's been in love with you for years, but you were clueless, as always."

"As always?"

"Yep. There have been plenty of women who would've tossed their loop around you if you'd noticed them . . ." Maverick's eyes filled with understanding. "Holy high heavens. The answer's as plain as day. You didn't notice anyone else because Maisy's been your whole world too."

Tanner started to shake his head in denial but then stopped himself. Hadn't he already admitted that part of the reason he had yet to move on was because of her?

"The real question is this." Maverick finished

buttoning his shirt and crossed his arms. "Why haven't you told her she's your whole world?"

"Guess I never let myself think about a future with her."

"Do you love her?"

It wouldn't hurt to admit it, would it? Especially because he was married to her. "Realized it during this last visit with her."

"But you didn't say so to her?"

He'd had the chance to share his feelings that last night together during the standoff with Lester. He could have said something this past week, like when she'd woken up from her fever. Or he could have told her during the short wedding ceremony. But he hadn't.

Slowly, he hung his head and shook it.

"Why?" Maverick's voice held a note of chastisement. "What's holding you back, Tanner?"

Maybe Maisy did look at him as if he was her world. But would that change eventually? "We want different things out of life."

Maverick just raised a brow.

"I won't make her happy."

This time Maverick snorted. "That's a bunch of cow dung. I ain't known Maisy long, but I can tell she don't need much to make her happy. Reckon having a man who loves her and ain't gonna leave her like her pa did is all she wants."

"But that's just it. My trapping takes me all over the mountains too."

"Take her with you."

Tanner's spinning thoughts slowed to a halt. Was the solution really that simple? She'd tagged along with him every day when he'd been staying with her. And if he was truly honest with himself, he'd loved spending the time together. Whether they'd been hiking silently or having a discussion, her companionship had filled him up. She'd seemed to enjoy being with him too.

Was it possible she would like going with him wherever he went? That they could work together?

"But that's not really the issue, is it?" Maverick's expression turned serious. "This ain't about her, Tanner. This is about you."

He started to protest, then he clamped his jaw closed.

Maverick was right. Tanner didn't really care all that much about his fur trapping or trail guiding. If he didn't do it anymore, he'd probably be fine. Sure, he loved the wilderness and always would. But he'd settled on the mountain-man life because he'd been restless and searching for a place to belong.

Maybe that restlessness and searching had stemmed from the fear he'd unleashed just a moment ago—the fear that nobody wanted him. Was it possible he'd even sabotaged his relationship with Maisy and had kept pushing her away so that he wouldn't have to face her rejection?

It was not only possible, it was true. He'd been afraid—and maybe still was—that if he allowed himself to get too close to her, she wouldn't really want him. Was she doing the same? Pushing him away to avoid getting hurt again by another man who was like her pa?

The fact was, her rejection by her pa was worse than anything he'd ever experienced. At least his parents hadn't willingly left him. They'd loved him enough to sacrifice themselves to save him and Ryder by hiding them in the secret compartment in the covered wagon.

But Maisy's pa hadn't loved her enough to sacrifice anything for her. Instead, Cleveland had chosen to walk out of his daughter's life and leave her behind. No wonder she'd run away.

Tanner buried his face in his hands and groaned. Instead of loving her above everything else and sacrificing for her the way she'd needed, all he'd done was hold her at arm's length. "I'm to blame. I pushed her away because of my own insecurities."

"Then it looks like you gotta make peace with those insecurities."

It was past time that he made peace with all that had happened, the same way Ryder had. Tanner knew he'd already come a long way. After all, he'd let go of his need to investigate who his family was. But he obviously had another step in the healing process, and that was the need to stop looking at himself as a nobody who didn't belong anywhere.

His past was behind him. He still had his whole life ahead of him. It was time to truly let himself belong to the Oakley family and also to make a new family of his own. He had a feeling his parents, watching him from heaven, would want him to be free from where he'd been stuck for so long and move on.

He couldn't think of anyone that he wanted to make a new family with more than Maisy. In fact, he couldn't think of anything that he'd ever want more. Because the truth was, no matter where he was or what he was doing, they could have a happy marriage if he just had the courage to let go of his past and all the baggage that came with it.

An urgent need began to pulse through him—the need to be with her, to have her by his side, and to never be apart ever again, even for just a minute. She was his whole life, his family, and his future. And he needed to let her know nothing else mattered but her.

As if sensing the inner turmoil, Maverick laid a hand on Tanner's shoulder and squeezed.

"I have to show her how much she means to me, Mav." He had to do something big, something that would show her he was different than her pa, something that would send a message loud and clear that he loved her more than anything or anyone else and that he'd sacrifice everything to have her, even his life.

"What do you want to do?" Maverick watched him expectantly.

The urge to rush out tonight pushed at Tanner. At the very least, he had to make sure she was someplace safe and secure. Even though she was a strong woman and could make her way anywhere just fine, especially if Smoke was nearby protecting her, she was still weak and vulnerable from her injury. He'd never rest if he didn't find out where she'd gone.

He stood, situated his gun belt more securely around his waist, then nodded at the door. "I need to locate her and make sure she's okay. But I'll wait until tomorrow to talk to her, after I have a plan in place for winning her back."

"I'll ride out with you." Maverick started tucking in his shirt.

Tanner was tempted to tell him to go back to his wife, but he knew Maverick would never listen, that he'd stay with him until the end. Just the way family did for each other.

He stuck out his hand for a handshake. "You're a good brother, Mav."

Maverick looked at his hand and then his face. Before Tanner realized it, Maverick was pulling him into a back-slapping embrace. "You're a good brother too, Tanner."

A new warmth settled deep inside Tanner. He'd held back a piece of himself from his family for too long. And it was time to give them all his love the same way they'd given him all of theirs.

As he headed out into the cold night with Maverick and crossed the ranch yard toward the barns, his gaze snagged on a wolf in the moonlight on a rise a short distance from the mare barn. Smoke was still here.

Tanner halted abruptly. That could only mean one thing. Maisy was still here too.

Smoke glanced Tanner's way as if to say hi, then he focused back on the mare barn.

Maverick had stopped beside him and noticed Smoke now too.

"Maisy's in the mare barn," Tanner whispered.

Maverick nodded. "Want me to go in and see where she's at?"

"Yes." Better Maverick than him. He was more than a little relieved that she hadn't ventured far yet, and he didn't want to take any chance that she'd take one look at him and this time really run away.

Maverick started forward, sauntering casually, as if he made a practice of browsing among the horses every night before going to bed.

"Make sure she doesn't realize you're checking up on her," Tanner whispered after him.

"I'll tell her you're waiting for her back in bed." Maverick tossed him a teasing grin. "Don't worry. I'll pretend I don't see her."

Tanner waited in the middle of the ranch yard, unable to move. He wanted to race into the barn, find Maisy, and pull her into his arms. But the next time he talked with her, he didn't want to have any more fumbling conversations where he said everything wrong and made a mess of their relationship.

He wanted to make things right between them and show her how much he loved her.

It didn't take Maverick more than five minutes or so before he moseyed out of the barn.

"She okay?" Tanner's question came out breathless with the anxiety that was closing up his lungs.

Maverick was chewing on a piece of hay, twirling it between his teeth. "Yep. She's fast asleep in a big pile of hay in the empty stall."

"Does she look all right?"

"So comfortable I doubt you'll get her out."

Tanner let the tension ease from his shoulders.

Maverick clamped him on the shoulder. "She might just decide to make that stall your new home."

"Guess I'll have to tempt her with something better." As soon as the words left Tanner's mouth, he straightened, and his thoughts began to race with an idea, the possible beginning of a plan to win her over.

If he went through with it, he'd need Clementine to come out to the barn in the morning and buy him a little time by stalling Maisy from heading wherever she might try to go next.

His heart pattered with new excitement. He wanted to leave Maisy with no doubt how he felt. He just hoped he could do it.

20

At the squeak of a nearby door, Maisy awoke with a start. Though the horse stall was shrouded in shadows, low light filtered in from the lanterns that were hanging from the rafters in the center aisle.

And sunlight. Beams were slanting in through the cracks in the boards nearby, which meant it was way past dawn, and she'd missed her chance to sneak off before anyone was awake.

"Shoot." She'd had every intention of borrowing a horse to ride into town last night. But when she'd finally made it to the barn, she'd been winded from the effort and her shoulder had ached from the exertion. So she'd stumbled into an empty stall, telling herself that she'd rest for a little while before heading out.

But a little while had turned into hours, and she'd wasted the cover of darkness and still hadn't made her escape.

Surely by now Tanner had realized that she'd run off and left the pillows and blankets under the covers. So where was he? She'd expected him to discover her absence last night, sound the alarm, and race off to search for her.

But she hadn't heard his voice or any horses coming and going from the ranch.

Either he hadn't noticed she was gone, or her disappearance hadn't bothered him as much as she'd thought—hoped—it would. Or maybe he'd ridden off while she'd been asleep, and the commotion hadn't awoken her. That was possible, since she'd been exhausted.

She pushed up from the hay pile where she'd buried herself for warmth, and the cool air nipped at her cheeks. Her body was stiff, and her shoulder ached, but otherwise, she wasn't any worse off after sleeping a night in the barn.

She sat up higher, hay sticking to her hair and face and wool coat. She blew at a strand hanging over one eye but only managed to make it flop down and tickle her nose.

A sneeze escaped before she could cover it.

She froze and waited, listening for any voices or sounds that would indicate someone being in the barn. By this time of the morning, she guessed there were workers who'd been in and out of the barn to tend to all the mares and foals.

So how would she be able to sneak away now? Especially without being detected. Would she have to wait another whole day before attempting to leave again?

She flopped back down and let out a frustrated huff. A hungry growl rumbled low in her belly, reminding her she'd skipped eating most of yesterday because she'd been too upset by the turn of events. And now she was famished.

At a soft tap against the stall door, she glanced around frantically, trying to find a place to hide. Should she burrow into the hay? But even as she lifted a hand of hay and tossed it over her head, she realized the silliness of her action. She'd never be able to bury herself thoroughly enough. And obviously, whoever was knocking knew she was there. Why else would he knock?

Was it Tanner? Had he tracked her to the stall? Of course he had. There likely wasn't any place where she could go that he wouldn't be able to track her.

She sat up straighter and shook her head, her hair having loosened from her single plait and become full of hay too. No doubt she looked as ragged as she felt. But what did it matter? She didn't need to impress Tanner anymore. Not that she'd ever wanted to impress him before.

That wasn't entirely true. From the first day she'd met him, she'd always wanted him to notice her and think she was pretty and find her attractive. And in the most forbidden of her secret dreams, she'd always imagined him wanting to be with her too.

What she'd never imagined was that he'd have to marry her in order to save his life. And even hours later, she was still mortified by the whole ordeal.

The door opened a crack.

She covered her face with her hands. She was being silly and behaving like a child, but apparently she would have to face Tanner now whether she was ready or not.

"Maisy?" A woman's voice greeted her.

Maisy shifted her fingers so she could peek between them and found herself peering up at Clementine.

"Thought I heard you stirring in here," the young woman said with a smile. She was attired in a pretty, dark-green skirt and matching bodice, much too fancy for mucking stalls and shoveling feed into troughs.

In fact, in the few interactions Maisy'd had with Clementine, she'd gotten the impression that the woman wasn't interested in the horses or the ranch the same way Hazel and Maverick were. Instead, she spent most of her time at home either baking or making the candy that she sold in town.

Clementine had her pretty blond hair pulled up into a knot and a green hat perched on top, accentuating the reddish tones that highlighted the hair. She was such a lovely woman, so feminine and polished compared to Maisy.

Maisy moved her hands from her face, pretending to wipe the hay off her cheeks as she did so. "I was just resting for a bit out here because . . ." Maisy fumbled to find a plausible reason for staying in the barn. "Because even though Tanner and me are married, I didn't wanna share the bed with him."

As soon as the excuse slipped out, Maisy could feel her cheeks heating.

Clementine's brows lifted above her rounded eyes.

"What I mean is that me and Tanner aren't gonna stay married." There. She'd said it. The truth. Maybe she didn't need to run away. Maybe she just had to be honest and tell everyone she didn't intend to hold Tanner to his vows—not when her pa had forced him to say them at knife point.

"My pa was a brute, and he shouldn't have made Tanner marry me. That's all there is to it." Her pa had been more than a brute. He'd been obnoxious and overbearing. Her chest squeezed with the same pain that had been holding her captive since yesterday, since he'd told her goodbye and ridden away.

"Tanner looks like he had a fight with a meat cleaver."

"He does?" Maisy had avoided him since the unfortunate wedding. But she could only imagine how cut up he was. A burst of anger rose up to swirl with the pain. "Good riddance to my pa. I hope I never have to see him again."

"I heard the whole story from Maverick." Clementine's gaze strayed around Maisy's face, lingering there tenderly. "I'm just sorry I had to miss the wedding."

"You're lucky you weren't there." The ache in Maisy's chest shifted into her throat. "It was awful. And I feel terrible that it happened." She'd cried too many tears to count yesterday about everything—about losing her pa, about losing Tanner, even about losing Nelly. It had been the day to think sad thoughts and wallow in her despair.

But she couldn't go on like that. She was too strong to let everything destroy her. She had to find a way to push forward and make a new life. Maybe that wouldn't be with Ma's family in Minnesota, but she'd figure out something.

"Well, I for one am happy to see that Tanner is finally married." Clementine's smile widened, making her utterly vivacious and enchanting.

"Finally?"

"He was too obsessed with finding his family and never made the time for a woman in his life." Clementine paused and pressed a finger to her lips, as if in thought. "Or maybe he already had you and wasn't interested in anyone else."

"He didn't have me. We're just friends, that's all."

"Sure. Just friends."

Maisy knew she wasn't fooling Clementine any more than she was fooling herself. Tanner was much more than a friend. "It doesn't matter. I'm not staying married to him, because he'll end up leaving me just like my pa did."

"Oh, honey," Clementine said with a wave of her hand. "I know Tanner pretty well, and he's the last man who will leave you."

"He's a wanderer."

"Only because he hasn't found a home yet."

"And because he loves the wilderness."

She shrugged. "He needs a good woman to wrangle his heart, and then he'll be just fine."

Maisy wished that were true, but he'd already rejected her once. "Men like him never settle down."

Clementine paused, her smile fading. "Not all men are like your pa, Maisy. And Tanner is one of the most dependable and trustworthy men you'll ever meet."

Maisy couldn't disagree. Tanner had always visited regularly, had always looked out for her, and he'd been the one to rescue her on the cliff and help her bury Nelly.

"You know what I think?" Clementine continued. "Tanner's always been hesitant to get into a relationship because when he does, he wants to be there and make it forever."

Was that why he was hesitant about committing? "I don't know."

"I do. Tanner once lost his family, and he never wants to lose another."

He had always been angry at Pa for leaving her and

Nelly behind, had always insinuated that he'd never do that to his women. Was it possible she'd been too quick to assume he'd be like her pa and now needed to give him a chance to prove he was different?

Longing stirred deep inside. Oh, how she ached for him to be different. But how could she set aside her mistrust of men?

She doubted there was an easy way to let go of her hurt and all the rejection she'd experienced from her pa, but she guessed that was the first step. If she wanted to learn to trust again, she had to heal her old wounds.

"Tanner never would have married you yesterday if he was planning to walk away," Clementine said, softening her voice so that it was reassuring.

"Tanner never would have married me yesterday if my pa hadn't been torturing him with a hunting knife."

"Not true. Maverick said Tanner could have gotten free from your pa."

"Pa would have killed him—"

"Maverick saw Tanner pull out his revolver but then put it back."

Maisy's heartbeat gave a hop.

"No one made Tanner marry you. He chose to. Maverick would have intervened if he'd sensed Tanner wasn't willing."

Had Tanner really chosen to marry her? Had he wanted it? Maisy's heartbeat hopped again, this time faster. Could she really allow herself to hope Tanner cared enough about her to make the choice to marry her?

Clementine extended a hand. "Come on. Let's get you inside and get you something to eat and something clean to wear."

An objection pushed to the tip of Maisy's lips. She couldn't stay at the Oakleys' any longer than she already had. But Clementine was already helping her to her feet and tugging her forward.

Maisy was halfway across the ranch yard before she halted. What was she doing? She wasn't ready to see Tanner. Not yet.

Clementine arched a brow at her. "What's wrong?"

She didn't want to interact with him looking as though she'd just wrestled with a goat in a gunnysack. "Maybe I should clean up before . . . well, before going inside."

A twinkle lit up Clementine's eyes. "Would it help to know that Tanner's not home right now?"

"He's not?" Maisy scanned the log home, then the ranch yard.

Clementine started tugging her toward the house again, and Maisy didn't resist this time.

"Where is he?"

"He had to run an errand."

Maisy halted again at the base of the porch steps. "Is he out looking for me?"

Clementine laughed again. "Do you really think Tanner wouldn't have found you by now?"

Of course he'd easily tracked her to the barn. "So he left without wanting to talk to me?" She obviously had a different standard for Tanner than for herself, since she'd been willing to run away without talking to him just yesterday.

She'd been wrong to do so. And even though she wanted to blame her lapse in judgment on all the emotion that had overwhelmed her yesterday, she couldn't make excuses. She should have talked with Tanner before sneaking out of the house.

Clementine didn't answer her question. How could she?

With a sigh, Maisy followed Clementine inside. She allowed Clementine to help her into clean garments, borrowing a pretty blue skirt and matching bodice that apparently Clarabelle had left behind when she'd gotten married. Clementine also combed and styled Maisy's hair, so that when Maisy looked into the mirror above the dressing table in Clementine's room, she was surprised at how grown-up she looked. And even pretty.

They were just finishing up a cup of coffee and toast at the large kitchen table when the rumbling of wheels in the ranch yard announced a visitor.

Clementine arose with an eager smile and rushed to the window. As she swept aside the curtain and peered out, her smile faded, and her forehead wrinkled. "What on earth is Grady Worth doing here?"

Maisy pushed away from the table and stood, trying to quell the disappointment that the newcomer wasn't Tanner returning from his errands. Now that she was gussied up and had prepared herself for talking to him, she needed to do it before she lost her resolve.

Clementine spun away from the window and hurried into the large front room of the cabin. Maisy followed more slowly, hesitating by one of the sofas.

Clementine reached the front door and halted. She smoothed a hand down her skirt before tucking a loose strand of hair back away from her face. Were her cheeks flushed now? Or had they been that way before?

Maybe Grady Worth was someone special to Clementine.

Clementine stared at the door, folding her arms across her chest, then relaxing them by her side only to fist them on her hips in the next instant.

When several quick thuds resounded, Clementine jumped and then smoothed her skirt again before reaching for the doorknob. She cleared her throat, bent her brows into a frown, then threw open the door.

A stocky, well-built fellow stood on the porch. He wore a Stetson over his dark-brown hair, shadowing his eyes and a handsome, clean-shaven face. He didn't seem to be surprised to see Clementine any more than she was surprised to see him.

"What are you doing here, Grady Worth?" Clementine asked, her voice laced with a hostility that Maisy hadn't expected.

"Hello to you too." Grady's answer was casual and almost irritatingly cheerful. "Nice weather we're having, wouldn't you say?"

"It would only be nice if it rained ice—specifically on you."

Grady snorted. "No need—not when I have to face your frigidness. You've already frozen me with just one look."

"Good." She continued to glare at him. "Now, tell me what you want. I'm busy and don't have the time to waste speaking to you."

Maisy couldn't keep from gasping at what was turning out to be a brutal exchange between the two.

Clementine's green eyes swung to her, followed by Grady's dark ones—which were thankfully filled with humor and not anger.

"I came to collect Maisy," Grady said with a nod in her direction.

"Why?" Clementine's question was sharp.

"Because I want to carry her away and marry her."

"She's already married to Tanner."

"I know that."

"Then what do you want with her?"

Maisy finally closed her mouth. She'd never witnessed grown adults acting like ill-mannered children, but Clementine and Grady were sure coming close.

Grady's expression still remained casual, but there was an intensity in his expression that he couldn't hide. "Tanner hired me to bring Maisy into town."

21

Maisy released her hold on the sofa and took a step toward the door. Tanner had hired Grady Worth? To bring her into town? "Is Tanner okay?"

"He's just fine." Grady tossed her a smile. "He wants to talk to you and thought it would be easier on your shoulder if you rode in one of my carriages."

Her stomach clenched. What did Tanner want to talk about? Before she could voice the question, Clementine sniffed at Grady as though she'd had all she could stand of talking to him. Then she turned and smiled brightly at Maisy—so brightly that the contrast from a moment ago was disarming and told Maisy all she needed to know: Clementine and Grady were attracted to each other but were also enemies.

Maisy guessed it was an interesting story, and she wanted to hear more about it, but at the moment, her nerves were pulling even tighter, tangling her insides.

What if Tanner was at the lawyer's office having divorce or annulment papers drawn up? She wouldn't blame him if he was.

But even as the doubts reared up and threatened to make her knees buckle, she tried to cling to Clementine's assurances from the barn. Tanner was one of the most dependable men she'd ever met. Tanner could've stopped the wedding and wouldn't have married her if he'd been planning to walk away.

All the ride into Breckenridge, cushioned among blankets, she kept reminding herself of one thing in particular that Clementine had told her: not all men were like her pa. She suspected that would be a truth she'd have to continue to teach herself.

But the reality was, she loved Tanner more than life, and she was willing to do the hard work to try to trust him. In fact, she loved him more than her safety, security, and stability, and she'd go anywhere and do anything in order to be with him. If that made her like her ma and Nelly, then so be it. Maybe loving unconditionally like them wasn't wrong, especially if it was with the right man.

Once they reached town, Grady directed the team onto a pleasant-looking side street with a few businesses but mostly newer homes. The carriage rolled down the gravelly street until Grady halted in front of a spacious home that was two stories tall with steep, gabled roofs, a turret rising from one side of the roof, intricately carved woodwork decorating the windows and gables, a large wraparound porch, and a wrought-iron fence surrounding the yard.

Perhaps they were picking up Tanner here. It was possible he was visiting with a friend or an associate over business matters.

She watched the front door of the house, waiting for him to make an appearance, but Grady swung open the carriage door and poked his head inside. "Ready?"

She hesitated, glancing at the imposing home. "Where's Tanner? I thought he wanted to talk to me."

"He's inside, waiting for you."

A strange tremor shook Maisy. She didn't want to assume the worst, but it was hard not to wonder what Tanner was thinking today. Especially since she'd shut him out of her life recently.

Grady helped her down and then walked with her up the front path to the porch, holding on to her elbow to steady her.

Maisy wanted to tell him she could make her way just fine without his help, but she bit back the words, knowing he was just trying to be a gentleman. At the door, she lifted her hand to knock, but before she could, the door opened, and Tanner was standing there wearing dark trousers and a matching vest and suit coat over a starched white shirt. His face was shaved, giving her a perfect view of his angular jaw and cheeks—and the cuts her pa had given him, which were red but thankfully not bad. He wasn't wearing a hat, and his hair was cut to his collar and combed back in smooth waves.

She drew in a sharp breath at how handsome he looked in his Sunday best. He cleaned up better than she ever could've imagined, and she liked this version of him almost as much as the rugged, mountain-man version.

How was it that in the few years she'd known him, she'd never seen him attired in a suit? In the mountains and on the ranch, he had no need for anything but work clothes. But of course he had a suit for church, weddings, and funerals. And he'd probably worn it a lot when he'd gone to New York City with Ryder.

But why today?

"I hope this isn't a lawyer's office, Tanner Oakley." She tried to glare at him, but she was still too overcome by how handsome he looked to get enough power behind the glare.

It was a good thing he'd never come up into the mountains looking like this. If he had, she wouldn't have been able to hold off kissing him for as long as she had.

A slow grin worked its way up his mouth, curling that perfect upper lip of his.

She couldn't look there. Wouldn't. Or she'd embarrass herself by throwing herself into his arms and dragging his mouth down to hers and kissing him right there in front of the whole house.

"No, this isn't a lawyer's office," he said with a nod of thanks to Grady before closing the front door. Tanner's suit coat stretched tight around his biceps and his shoulders and outlined his muscles and broad back. Suddenly, all she could think about was skimming her hands up and down those biceps and over his back.

She jerked her attention away from him. She. Could. Not. Touch. Him. At least, not yet. They had too much to talk about before she could let herself get carried away.

She glanced around the spacious front hallway with its light ivy-print wallpaper, the matching ivy-print rugs, and the framed pictures of what appeared to be dried flowers that had probably been picked locally.

Off to one side was a spacious front parlor, and she caught sight of a large desk in one corner. Off to the other side of the hallway was a dining room with an elegant table and chairs.

She expected to see the residents of the home stepping out of one of the rooms or at least coming down the wide carpeted stairway from the second floor. But the house was so quiet that she could hear Grady's carriage rumbling away.

"Where is everyone?" she whispered.

He quirked an eyebrow. "Everyone?"

"You know, the folks who live here."

His smile faded. "What would you say if I told you

that we're the folks who live here?"

She smacked him in the arm. "I'd say hush up!"

His expression turned tentative, and he grew quiet.

Her racing heart stuttered and then came to a stop. "What? You can't be serious." Her gaze swept over the lavish home once more, this time taking in the richness of it as well as the beauty. When she turned her attention back upon him, he was watching her face as though trying to gauge her reaction.

"Tanner?" Her voice trembled. What was he doing? "Don't fool around with me like this."

He reached for her hand, the one with her wedding band, and he touched it. "I'm not fooling around. This is me being completely serious, if you haven't noticed the suit and tie and everything."

Oh, she had noticed. That was for sure. But at the moment, she was too overcome by his announcement. "Why?" It was the only word she could think of, the only word that would come out.

He seemed to swallow hard, then fiddled with her wedding ring again. "I bought the house for you—for us."

"You bought it?" Her mind began to reel, dizzyingly, crazily.

"It's a pretty house in town," he said with a gentle smile, "with two stories and painted shutters. It doesn't have a swing on the front porch yet, but it does have a fenced-in backyard where you can put bird feeders and have the space to take care of baby animals."

Lord Almighty, have mercy. What kind of man would remember exactly what she'd said and then give it to her? Only Tanner Oakley. That's who. And she loved him for it, even if she couldn't accept his gift.

"The assayer used to live here," he continued. "He got arrested earlier in the year. After his wife moved, the house has been sitting empty with all the furnishings, so I asked around and offered to buy it."

"I don't understand. You love the wilderness—"

"No. I love *you*." The words came out impassioned and ended with a plea. He reached for her other hand now so that he was holding both. "I'm sorry I didn't say it that night in the cabin. Because I loved you then, and I was just too much of a coward to say it."

He loved her. The words sank in and shattered any resistance that was left—which hadn't been much. "I'm sorry I was a coward yesterday—"

"You don't have anything to be sorry for."

"That's not true. I'm stubborn and pushy and rash and—"

"And I love you." He spoke the words again, this time firmly. "You're all that matters. Not the wilderness or the mountains or the trapping."

"But that's where you're happy."

"As long as I have you and we're together, I'll be happy."

She shook her head. "No, I won't take you away from it. I can't—"

"You know I've been restless there and trying to sort out what's next. And even though I don't exactly know what I'll do, this is a start."

"A start?"

"I thought maybe over the winter I'd write a book—this time one I can send to a publisher, maybe the one Ryder is using for his history book."

Was she dreaming? Was this really happening to her? Tanner had just told her he loved her. That she was all that mattered. And he'd proven it to her by giving her what she'd dreamed about—a normal house and a normal life.

She couldn't keep from wavering, weak from her wound and now overwhelmed by everything.

His brow furrowed, and he scooped her up so that he was holding her against his chest. She knew she needed to protest, but she couldn't think straight.

"What's wrong, darlin'?"

"I can't let you give up everything for me, Tanner."

"But I want to—"

"Let's live in your cabin in the wilderness for part of the year and then stay here in our house in town for the other part."

He was watching her face, and she prayed he'd see the earnestness there.

"I love the wilderness too," she continued. "And I'll probably eventually miss it. So why not split our time?"

His eyes turned tender. "Thank you for offering. I appreciate it. But we don't have to figure it out today."

"Okay." She cupped his cheek. "Just promise that whatever we do or wherever we go, we'll always stay together."

"That is definitely one promise I'll be able to keep." He grinned. "I'll never let you out of my sight again."

His words were the assurance she'd needed and brought a rush of warmth to her heart. She couldn't keep from smiling in return. And she also couldn't keep from staring at his kissable upper lip. Had they talked enough now that she could allow herself to get carried away?

Too bad if they hadn't. She was gonna kiss him anyway.

She slid her hand to the back of his neck and dragged him down. At the same time, she lifted up and captured his lips with hers. They were warm and soft and slick. Oh, he felt so good. So, so good. She just wanted to kiss him and never do anything else ever again.

She could feel him still grinning against her even as he pressed into her.

"What?" she asked, pulling back.

His dark eyes swept over her face, the heat in them lighting her on fire. "I love when you do that."

"Do what?"

"Kiss me in that bossy way of yours."

"Good." She gave him a quick but hard kiss. "You'll need to get used to it, because I intend to do it often."

He chuckled and in the next instant meshed his mouth with hers with a powerful surge that left no doubt he was just as bossy when it came to kissing and that he would demand as much as she did.

She may have wrangled the wandering rancher, but he'd wrangled her heart too.

"Coming!" Tanner called as he raced down the stairway, stuffing his arms into the sleeves of his flannel shirt.

The knocking on the front door was persistent and had only gotten louder instead of going away as he'd hoped.

He was being selfish. He was well aware of that fact. But he was a newlywed enjoying his bride this week, and he hated any and all interruptions.

Thankfully, there hadn't been many since he and Maisy had moved into their new house five days ago, the day after their wedding. Maverick and Hazel had stopped by once. Clementine had brought them food a couple of times. And a messenger had come with a telegram from Ryder, congratulating him on the marriage—in response to the telegram Tanner had sent to him.

One night he and Maisy had also been awakened by scratching on the back door. They'd gone down to find

Smoke sitting in the backyard. They weren't sure how he'd been able to sneak into town without being seen, but somehow he'd managed.

Maisy had hugged and kissed the wolf and invited him inside, but Smoke had just paced toward the back fence. He'd paused and looked at Tanner as if to admonish him to take good care of Maisy, then he'd peered at Maisy with his beautiful golden eyes for a long moment. In the next instant, he'd jumped the fence and disappeared . . . and they hadn't seen him since.

Over the past few days, they'd speculated as to where Smoke had gone and what he would do next. Tanner guessed the wolf sensed that Maisy no longer needed him now that she was married and had someone to take care of her, but Maisy thought Smoke was ready to go find a mate of his own.

Whatever the case, Maisy had taken the wolf's leaving much better than Tanner had expected. She'd told him again, as she had in the past, that whenever she rescued wild animals, she did so with the intention of releasing them into the wild where they belonged. She claimed Smoke was back where he belonged too. For better or worse, he would have to survive without Maisy.

Tanner began to hastily button his shirt while trying to tuck it into his trousers with only one suspender holding them up. His feet were bare and his hair mussed, but he didn't care. Once he sent away whoever was at the door, he was going up and crawling right back into bed with Maisy, and he didn't care that it was the middle of the day.

The knocking paused for just a moment before resuming even louder, if that were possible.

Tanner slipped another button through a hole, making that a total of three that partially covered his bare chest. Then he unlocked the door and swung it wide.

A middle-aged man in a dark suit paused with his fist ready to knock again, gave Tanner a once-over, then tsked. Without a word, he pulled a monocle out of his pocket, placed it over one eye, and then peered through it at Tanner as if he were a rare document he was reading.

"May I help you?" Tanner asked, trying not to be brusque. But the man didn't look familiar—no one Tanner had ever seen in Summit County.

"Tanner Oakley, I presume?" With his gloved hands, the man took hold of Tanner's chin and shifted his head sideways while he continued his inspection through the monocle.

"Yes, I'm Tanner." Tanner took a step back, breaking the man's grip, having reached his short limit on being manhandled by a stranger. "Who are you?"

The man tucked the single glass back into his pocket and then slipped out a folded stack of papers. "I'm Mr. Warner, the best private investigator in Boston, dare I say on the entire East Coast."

Obviously this man had learned about Tanner's previous investigations into his family and was now stepping forward to offer to do the job—and trying to prove his credentials for taking over the case.

"I'm sorry, Mr. Warner"—Tanner began to close the door—"but I'm not hiring another investigator. I'm done with that."

Mr. Warner placed a surprisingly strong hand against the door to keep it from shutting and pinned a severe gaze on Tanner. "You don't need to hire me since I've already been hired . . . by your grandfather."

Every function in Tanner's body crashed to a halt, and silence descended. What was this fellow saying? What could he possibly mean? "I don't have a grandfather." He said the only logical thing.

"As a matter of fact, you do have a grandfather, and his name is Donald Hart."

Donald Hart. Donald. A tremor raced through Tanner. Donny—Donald—was the name he'd had long ago when he'd been but an infant. Did he have some connection with Donald Hart?

Mr. Warner held Tanner's gaze. "Mr. Hart has been looking for his daughter's missing sons for at least two decades."

"His daughter?"

"Your mother, Sarah."

A rush of emotion swelled in Tanner's chest. Lord in

heaven above. Sarah was the name Ryder had remembered, the one he thought belonged to their mother. "How can you be sure Mr. Hart's daughter Sarah is my mother?"

Mr. Warner unfolded the papers in his hand, then took out his monocle again. "I've been keeping meticulous records for years, and all the details I've collected confirm that you are her son. Besides, the family resemblance to your father is quite evident."

"Hawthorne?" Tanner threw out the other name that Ryder had recalled.

Mr. Warner riffled through the documents. "Yes, Hawthorne Bertram."

Bertram. Tanner let the family name sift through his mind, testing it for any familiarity. But it didn't resonate, not any more than the given names.

Mr. Warner pulled out a photograph from among the stack. It was small, no bigger than the size of his palm. He turned it around, then extended it.

Tanner reached for it, surprised to find that his fingers were trembling. As he took it and held it up, he felt as if he were looking into a mirror. The face in the picture was young and carefree and full of life. The dark-brown hair, brown eyes, angular lines, and even the unsmiling mouth were all like his.

The emotion swirling inside Tanner pushed higher into his throat and cut off any response he could give to

Mr. Warner. There really were no words needed.

The man in the photograph was undeniably his father.

Of course, not everything was identical. The man had a crooked nose, as if it had once been broken. And he had a mole on one cheek and sported a dark and dashing mustache. He was attired in a suit that a wealthy gentleman might wear, with a cravat about his neck and a pocket-watch chain dangling from his coat.

Hawthorne Bertram. What kind of man had he been?

The hints of memories that Tanner had had from time to time had always made him believe his father and mother had been loving. And now he'd finally know the truth.

"Tell me about Hawthorne."

Mr. Warner skimmed down through his notes and halted on a paragraph of scribbled writing. "Hawthorne was a titled Englishman who was visiting in Boston when he met Sarah."

A titled Englishman? Tanner's fingers began to shake even more.

"He met Sarah Hart in 1852, and they were married in 1853 against the wishes of both of their parents."

"Against the wishes?"

"Your grandfather, Mr. Hart, is . . ." Mr. Warner pursed his lips for a moment. "Well, let us just say that Mr. Hart is a very wealthy man, and at the time, he had other aspirations for his only child."

"What aspirations?"

"For her to marry a very wealthy friend of his who also happened to be much older than her."

"And so she ran off with my father instead?"

"It was more complicated than that. She was grieving the recent loss of Mrs. Hart, and so was Mr. Hart. Without Mrs. Hart there to intervene, the situation only deteriorated."

"And Hawthorne's family?"

"Of course, your paternal grandfather, Lord Bertram, wasn't opposed to the Harts' fortune. But without the offer of a dowry, which Mr. Hart refused to give, they weren't willing to proceed with the union."

The information sounded like something from a novel, and Tanner could hardly take it all in.

Mr. Warner paged forward, peered through his monocle, and spoke again. "Without the support of either family, the newly married couple moved to Buffalo, New York, where Hawthorne worked for the railroad. They had their first child in 1854, a son named Edward after Hawthorne's father."

"Ryder thought his given name was Edward."

Mr. Warner continued as if he hadn't heard Tanner. "Sarah had a second son in 1856 named Donald after her father. They moved to Ohio in 1857, where Hawthorne continued to work for the railroad. Finally, in 1859, with the discovery of gold in Colorado, they decided to travel west and make their fortune."

Tanner could hardly believe he was having this conversation with Mr. Warner and hearing about his family. The information was everything he'd always wanted to know, but now that he had Maisy, it didn't seem quite as important as it once had.

"When Mr. Hart finally got the devastating news of Sarah's death, he also learned that the two boys hadn't been found among the dead. However, since months had already passed, he was left with no clues as to what had become of them."

If Tanner had harbored any doubts about Mr. Warner's story, he no longer did. Everything matched exactly with the little he knew. Even the dates of birth of Sarah's sons lined up with his and Ryder's ages.

If both of his parents had come from wealthy families, then it was no wonder that he'd never been able to find any information during his own investigations. He'd centered his search among simple folks, working-class people, even the immigrants who'd traveled west seeking new opportunities. He'd never considered the possibility that his parents' story had been completely different.

"Did Sarah play the violin?"

Mr. Warner glanced up from the papers, his eyes showing surprise. "Yes, she was a very skilled violinist. How did you know?"

"I have vague recollections of someone playing a violin."

"No doubt it was her."

The biggest question was still nagging Tanner. "How did Mr. Hart—how did you—track me down?"

Mr. Warner flipped to the last page of his stack and peered down at several newspaper articles that had been clipped and spread out over the sheet. One was circled and had scribbled notes beside it. Mr. Warner focused his monocle on it. "I read your advertisement in the *Boston Post* four weeks ago."

Tanner had been in New York City four weeks ago with Ryder. And Genevieve had been the one to suggest putting advertisements into major newspapers across the country. With her help, Tanner had crafted a short notice.

He peered at it now on the sheet in front of Mr. Warner: *Seeking family. Edward (25) and Donald (23), sons of Sarah and Hawthorne, were orphaned in a wagon-train attack on the Oregon Trail in 1859. Send information to Tanner Oakley at High Country Ranch in Breckenridge, Colorado.*

Mr. Warner was staring at the advertisement too. "It was a miracle to find this."

"I'd given up my own search," Tanner admitted, "and this was the last thing I did, the last thing I ever planned to do."

Mr. Warner looked up at Tanner with serious eyes. "It's a heaven-sent blessing. Your grandfather is dying, and it is his greatest wish to meet you and your brother before he passes. You must travel to Boston with me."

Tanner's heart squeezed with new hope. "When do we leave?"

23

Tanner held Maisy's hand too tightly, but she didn't seem to mind. She just laced her fingers more securely in his and leaned her head against his shoulder.

The butler had already taken their coats as well as Ryder's and Genevieve's. Now they were all waiting in the spacious entryway room outside the parlor of Donald Hart's Boston home.

As one of the largest homes in Boston, the mansion took up at least half the block with its extensive gardens and wooded area, sitting well back from the street, behind the tall iron fences that surrounded the complex. The front gate had only been opened to them when the guard there had confirmed their names and appointment with Mr. Hart.

Tanner pressed a kiss against Maisy's head, thankful once again they were both alike in their need to be constantly together. They hadn't been apart from each other since the day they'd moved into their home in Breckenridge two weeks ago, and he hoped they would never have to spend a day or night separated.

They'd arrived in New York City by train two days ago and had stayed with Ryder and Genevieve. Tanner had already telegrammed Ryder with some of the news he'd learned but had shared the rest once they were together. Mr. Warner had been with them, having been tasked by Mr. Hart not to leave them until he delivered them to his home in Boston.

Early this morning, they'd all boarded a train bound for Boston. Now Mr. Warner was in the parlor with Mr. Hart, having asked to go ahead to prepare the dying man for the reunion.

Ryder had left his baby back in New York City with a nursemaid, and now he had his arm around Genevieve and was leaning on her as if he needed her strength every bit as much as Tanner needed Maisy's.

Tanner caught Ryder's gaze. His brother's brown eyes and brown hair were the same dark shade as his, but Ryder was broader and taller. And much quieter and more contemplative. He was attired in a dark suit—one of the tailored outfits he'd acquired since moving to New York City. In fact, Tanner hadn't seen Ryder in anything but the fancy suits since his move there. But Ryder seemed at home in them, as if he'd been born to wear them.

Maybe he had.

Tanner still couldn't grasp the concept that their father had been an English lord. Mr. Warner had filled them in on more details about their father's family. Apparently they could trace their lineage back for generations, almost all the way to William the Conqueror. Upon hearing that, Ryder had pulled out a history book from among his collection and given Tanner a lesson on the Norman conquest.

Hawthorne Bertram had been the first-born son of Lord Bertram and had been the heir apparent in line to inherit his title and estates. He'd been a prolific writer, with several published books under a pen name, and he'd loved to travel and research for his novels.

Upon Hawthorne's death, Lord Bertram's second son had become the heir presumptive and still was. Mr. Warner declared that Ryder was technically now the heir apparent of Lord Bertram as the oldest son of the oldest son, but Ryder had shaken his head in his usual gruff way and declared that he had no desire to pursue anything from their father's family.

When Mr. Warner had insinuated that Mr. Hart had been relieved to find direct heirs of his fortune, both Tanner and Ryder had indicated that they wanted nothing from the older man. They both had enough to support themselves financially—especially Ryder, since Genevieve was a wealthy heiress and spoiled him with more than he needed.

Even so, Mr. Warner had been firm that Mr. Hart had already had his will rewritten and that everything would go to the two of them after his death.

Tanner didn't care about the will and wasn't afraid to tell Mr. Warner so.

The truth was, all that mattered was finally knowing their family's history. And it was even more special that they would have the opportunity today to meet at least one of their grandfathers, their mother's father.

Maisy pulled back slightly from him so that she could peer up at him, her pretty face earnest and her blue-green eyes filled with concern. She was attired in one of Genevieve's fashionable gowns of a cream color, which made her red hair appear a richer red-brown and her skin sun-toasted. The gown was tight fitting, molding to Maisy's body and leaving very little to the imagination.

He was having a hard time keeping his hands from roving over her. He longed to skim every inch of her body and kiss every inch of her skin, but he'd had to satisfy himself all day with stolen touches and kisses, her eyes promising much more later when they were alone.

He could see that Ryder's hands were all over Genevieve too and that she seemed to melt into him every chance she had. But that wasn't anything new.

"Are you ready?" Ryder asked gravely.

For so long Tanner had dreamed about a moment

like this. But now that it was here and he'd finally made peace with the past, his whole existence didn't depend on the outcome of today's meeting. Yes, he hoped to spend some time getting to know this grandfather. And yes, he planned to stay in Boston as long as he could, even through the whole winter if his grandfather lived that long and wanted him around.

Mr. Warner had confided that Mr. Hart had a bad heart, which was causing him to be weak and fatigued as well as to have shortness of breath, swelling in his limbs, and irregular heartbeats.

Tanner had discussed the situation with Maisy, and they'd both agreed that they had nothing tying them to Breckenridge and could come and go from there as they pleased. So they wouldn't be disappointed if they weren't able to make it back to the high country before the winter snow filled the mountain passes.

Even so, Tanner didn't know what to expect from Mr. Hart. If the gentleman had once cast out his only child because she'd chosen to spend her life with someone he didn't approve of, then he was likely a difficult man. Perhaps he'd changed or even softened some. That's what hardships often did to people.

Regardless, Tanner intended to make the most of the opportunity to meet this relative, get to know him, and spend as much time as possible with him. But if none of that worked out the way he hoped, he'd still walk away a happy man because, in the end, he had a woman he loved and his whole life ahead of him with her.

The parlor door opened, and the butler slipped through. Attired in a spotless dark suit with a bow tie, tailcoat, and gloves, he bowed his head politely, then waved them inside. "Mr. Hart is ready."

Ryder nodded at Tanner to enter ahead of him.

"You sure?" Tanner asked.

"You were the one who never gave up on finding family." Ryder's voice was gruff with emotion. "You should meet him first."

Tanner nodded his thanks, then with Maisy on his arm as beautiful and vivacious as always, he entered the parlor. It being the end of October, the evening light was already waning, but the room was lit with a large fire on the hearth, and each elegant globe lantern on each elegant pedestal table glowed with warmth. With walls papered in muted blues and greens, the room was impressively decorated with imported rugs and vases, richly carved dark furniture, and gilded frames and crystal candleholders.

It was everything he would have expected in a house like this.

In a comfortable-looking wing chair positioned near the fire, a gentleman sat with his feet perched on a stool and a thick blanket covering his legs. A small dog was curled on his lap, and it lifted its head as Tanner started toward them holding Maisy's hand.

The man didn't appear overly old. His hair was a light brown with hints of gray. His face was strong and purposeful. And he held himself with a confidence and pride that likely came from years of being someone wealthy and important.

His gaze, however, was much less certain as he locked in on Tanner, studying him intently, not even once glancing at Maisy.

As Tanner halted in front of the older man, he wasn't sure what to do. Should he wait for Mr. Hart to say something first? Or should he initiate a handshake? Without giving himself the chance to overthink, he offered a smile. "Grandfather?"

Immediately, tears welled in the man's eyes. He didn't even make an effort to blink them back and instead let them begin to trickle down his cheeks. He studied Tanner's face for another moment. Then he held out a hand.

Tanner didn't hesitate. He took the offer, and tears welled in his own eyes at the realization that he was connecting with his family—that in some ways, by touching his grandfather he was touching his mother and father and all that he'd once lost.

"Donald?" Grandfather's voice wobbled with emotion.

Tanner hesitated. He'd figured his family would

probably want to call him by his given name, Donny. But the more he'd thought about it, the more he'd realized that he was no longer Donny. He was Tanner—a man forged by all the hardships and heartaches he'd experienced.

"I go by Tanner now. And this is my wife Maisy." He tugged her forward now too. "We're pleased to meet you."

Grandfather's tears flowed faster. And instead of shaking Tanner's hand, he drew Tanner down and wrapped his arms around him in an embrace.

Tanner hugged his grandfather back, relief loosening the tension that had been building all day. Things were going to be okay. Maybe even more than okay.

"I'm sorry," Grandfather whispered brokenly. "I'm so sorry, Tanner."

Tanner pulled back.

Grandfather held him with surprising strength. "All that you went through is my fault."

"No, of course it's not—"

"Had I loved my daughter the way I should have, I wouldn't have lost her, and I wouldn't have lost you for so many years either."

The man's guilt edged each word, had probably edged his every action and word for years. Perhaps it was finally time for him to make peace with the past too. There was only one way to help the man start. "Don't worry,

Grandfather. I forgive you. And I love you."

Grandfather breathed in a quick breath that almost sounded like a sob. "You don't know how much I love you too and have waited for the chance to tell you."

Tears stung Tanner's eyes, and when he stood and took hold of Maisy's hand again, she squeezed his hard. Her eyes were glassy with tears, but she was smiling up at him—a smile filled with all the love she held for him.

As he smiled back, contentment settled inside him. The story of his family had been wrought with many strange twists and turns. He hadn't known where it would lead, had never expected it would bring him here to this moment. But he couldn't have asked for anything better.

He was learning that when life's stories were uncertain and difficult, happy endings were still possible. That with enough hard work and perseverance, even the darkest and most sorrowful of stories still had the potential for beauty.

He leaned down and kissed Maisy's head, his heart full with all he'd gained. He couldn't ask for more.

Dear Reader,

I hope you enjoyed this fourth book in the Oakley family saga, especially learning about Tanner and Ryder's history. It was fun to give them a different backstory and to have them both wrestle with being orphans. Their shared history and what they experienced together shaped them both in slightly different ways. I hope you're satisfied with their happily-ever-afters!

Even though we've wrapped up Ryder's and Tanner's stories, don't leave the high country quite yet. There's more to come with Clementine, who still has to find her true love. And yes, all throughout her siblings' stories, she and Grady have been fighting like cat and dog. So I hope you're ready for a fun enemies-to-lovers story in the fifth book of the High Country Ranch Series, with lots of adventure as well as lots of sizzling romance!

As always, I love hearing from YOU! If you haven't yet joined my Facebook Reader Room, what are you waiting for!? It's a great place to keep up-to-date on all my book releases and book news, as well as a fun place to connect with other readers and me.

Finally, the more reviews a book has, the more likely other readers are to find it. If you have a minute, please leave a rating or review. I appreciate all reviews, whether positive or negative.

Until next time . . .

Make sure you didn't miss out on any other books in the High Country Ranch series. Here's a complete list of all the books. They can be read as standalones, but they're even better read in order.

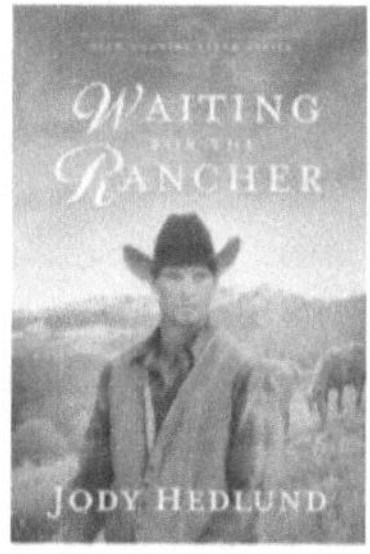

Waiting for the Rancher

Hazel Noble loves her job managing the mares at High Country Ranch. As the foaling season begins, she gets to spend even more time with the horses . . . and with her secret crush, Maverick Oakley, the owner of High Country Ranch and her brother Sterling's best friend. When Maverick unwittingly ruins Sterling's wedding, he goes from best friend to worst enemy. With the rift between their families, Maverick is faced with the possibility of losing Hazel, and he can no longer deny how much he's always cared about her.

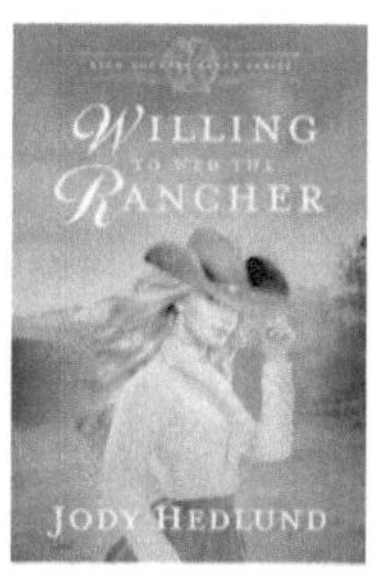

Willing to Wed the Rancher

Assistant schoolteacher Clarabelle Oakley has a hard time saying no. When Eric Meyer, widowed father of two of her young students, proposes to her, she botches her effort to tell him no and that she wants to marry for love, not convenience. Only days later, the unthinkable happens, and Clarabelle learns she's been given charge of Eric's children and his farm. Professor Franz Meyer arrives in Summit County, Colorado, to make peace with his estranged brother but discovers Eric is gone, leaving too many unanswered questions.

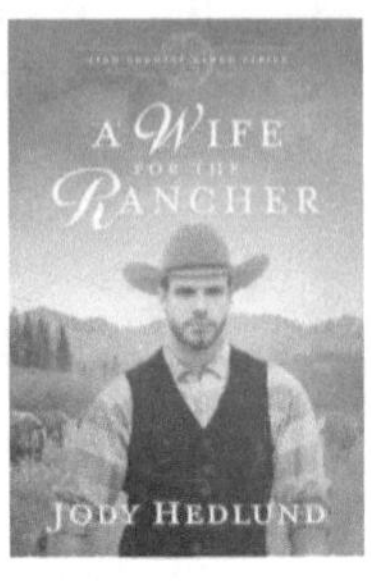

A Wife for the Rancher

Millionaire heiress, Genevieve Hollis, has everything she wants except one thing, freedom, because her guardian stepmother insists on overseeing every move she makes. When Genevieve sees a newspaper advertisement from a rancher seeking a mother for his baby, she jumps at the chance to escape. Ryder Oakley has suffered the repeated misfortune of losing the people he loves most, so now that he's a single father with a newborn baby, he's determined not to lose his son.

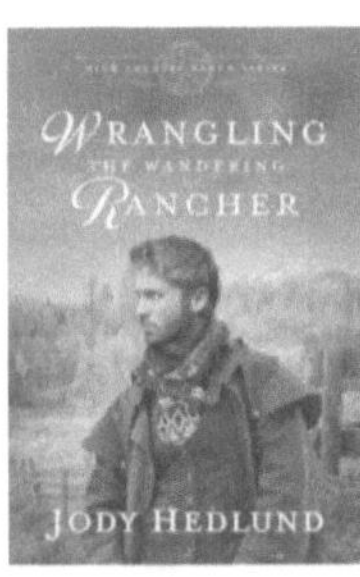

Wrangling the Wandering Rancher

Maisy Merritt has vowed she'll never marry a mountain man. Even though she loves the Colorado Rockies and the wild creatures she helps, she hates the way her pa's mountain-man ways take him away from his family. Maisy's ready to start a normal life, and that includes marrying a normal man. As a trapper and trail guide, Tanner Oakley lives a wandering life. He's decided that he's not husband material for any woman since he's so restless and unsettled.

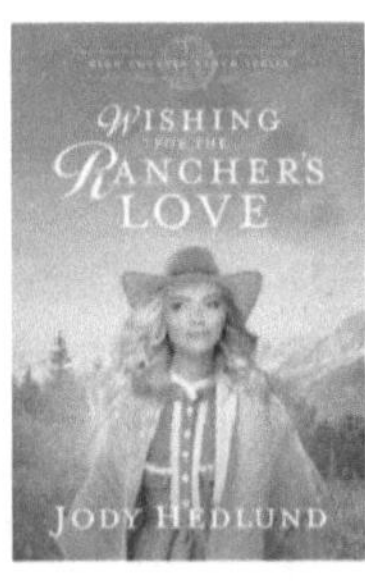

Wishing for the Rancher's Love

As the only one of her siblings who hasn't married, Clementine Oakley feels left behind. But she does her best to focus on her candy-making business in Worth's General Store. Giving and outgoing, she makes friends with everyone—except one person, the store owner's son . . . Grady Worth. Grady isn't sure why he can't get along with Clementine, but every time they're together, all they do is bicker. When his dad proposes a contest to encourage Grady to find love, Clementine is the last person he considers as an option.

Jody Hedlund is the bestselling author of more than fifty novels and is the winner of numerous awards. Jody lives in Michigan with her husband, busy family, and five spoiled cats. She writes sweet historical romances with plenty of sizzle.

A complete list of my novels can be found at jodyhedlund.com.

Would you like to know when my next book is available? You can sign up for my newsletter, become my friend on Goodreads, like me on Facebook, or follow me on Instagram.

Newsletter: jodyhedlund.com
Facebook: AuthorJodyHedlund
Instagram: @JodyHedlund